My Search for Ruth

My Search for Ruth

Anna Clarke

Richardson, Steirman & Black
NEW YORK

CHAPTER I

THE HEAD in the wall; that was the first of my memories. It had a grinning red face, surrounded by hair sticking up in all directions like Shockheaded Peter, and it shot out of the shadows by the side of the fireplace in my Aunt Bessie's little living-room and remained there twisting about as if it belonged to some monstrous being that was striving to break through the brown wallpaper and run rampant through the house, leaving in its wake a horror beyond what the mind could bear.

Of course it was a dream, but it was so vivid that it coloured all my waking hours and when in the evening I sat on a low stool in front of the burning coals, it seemed to me that my aunt's face, pink in the glow of the firelight, took on the appearance of the face in the dream.

'Can I switch the light on, Auntie?' I asked. 'I can't see my book.'

'Not just yet, Ruth,' she replied, working away at her knitting with eyes half closed. 'Uncle will be home soon.'

I thought we must be very poor, to have to sit in the twilight so long; it did not occur to me that my aunt might be nervous of the new electric light that had only recently been installed in the village. I turned back to my book. It was about King Arthur and the Knights of the Round Table, in large print and with coloured illustrations of castles and lakes and forests and shining knights on white horses. I peered closer to the page; when the coals flared up I could just see the words; they put beautiful pictures into my head, they were my protection against the hideous face of the dream.

But when the fire burned low I felt the coming of night and the return of the terror.

'Auntie!' I cried suddenly. 'Suppose there was a dragon living in the wall.'

She gave a little start; she had been dozing with her hands still grasping the knitting.

'A dragon – in the wall,' she repeated slowly. And then, in a brisker voice : 'Don't talk such nonsense, Ruth. You read too much, child. That's what's the matter with you. It puts ideas into your head.'

She began to knit again rapidly, shaking her head from time to time and saying, more to herself than to me : 'Uncle will be home soon. He can't be long now.'

'Auntie,' I said presently, after trying in vain to make out the words on the next page, 'where is my mummy?'

'Oh dear.'

She sighed deeply and then began to shake her head very quickly, in time with the jerky movements of her fingers as they knitted. She seemed to me very old and frail and I felt wicked for having upset her. Suppose she were to die! She must have been about sixty then, and I was seven and had heard people say that I was forward for my age. I didn't know what they meant, unless it was something to do with there being for me no 'backward', since everything that had happened to me before I found myself sitting by my aunt's fire was blurred and dim. The only things that were clear were the terrible dream and the memory of somebody very different from my aunt, who had been my mummy.

I longed for my aunt to talk about her but I dared not ask any more. I looked at my book again but could no longer make any sense out of the dim page. I seemed to be made of fear, every little bit of me. It wasn't from outside, it was right in myself, beating in my heart, breathing in and out in little pants. My eyes were fear, my ears were fear. Only my hands holding tight to the big heavy book were free of it, for the book was my only refuge, a world where fear was not.

In the little firelit room, quiet and still save for the busy needles and the chunky tick of the grandfather clock, my old auntie and I waited for our release. She must have been more alert than I was, for I did not hear the creak of the gate being opened, nor the faint crunch of bicycle wheels upon the gravel path.

'There he is,' she cried, whisking her knitting into the big canvas bag that hung from the arm of her chair. 'Run and meet him, Ruth. I'll soon have this kettle boiling again.'

She poked at the fire, amazingly vigorously for such a frail little old lady, and pulled the big black kettle nearer to the flames. I ran from the room into the narrow hall, pushed up the latch of the front door, which was only just within my reach, crept round the door and stood shivering for a moment on the step, overwhelmed by the great, cold, dark world of night. It was strange, mysterious and frightening, and yet at the same time it comforted me. The great wide world outside was my salvation, my escape from the horror within. And there were lights – the stars on this clear December evening, the faint glow from cottage windows, the oil-lamp on my uncle's bicycle which he was putting away in the shed.

I ran round to the side of the shed and hid myself so that I could jump out at him when he came out.

He flashed the bicycle lamp at me, making a great show of surprise.

'Why – if it isn't my little Ruthie.'

I clung to his hand. I was shivering with cold but I did

not want to go in. Fear was inside, right there by the warm
fire, by the hearth, at the very heart of things.

'Come on,' he said. 'There's a hungry man here – a man
who wants his tea.'

He was small, brown, and wrinkled, my old Uncle
Matthew, a sweet, crisp, ginger-nut of a man. He looked
after the gardens at a girls' school and I loved to hear him
talk about the young ladies there and wished I could see
them too.

'All in the dark!' he exclaimed as we came into the little
room. 'Why, what's the good of having the electric if you're
not going to use it?'

My aunt was stooping over the hearth, pouring boiling
water into the teapot.

'There's no need to waste it,' she said.

She spoke sharply, like someone who has been afraid
and is afraid no longer, but is still angry with the person
who has made her afraid. Somehow I understood all this,
although I was so young, and although I had no memories
and experience to draw upon, but it made me sad because
I loved my uncle.

'Draw the curtains, Ruth,' said my aunt in the same
snapping voice.

I did so, still not liking to shut out the great unknown
darkness where hope and promise lay, although with the
coming of my uncle fear had departed from the little
crowded room. The bare electric bulb that hung from the
ceiling cast light into every corner and the firelight faded to
nothingness.

For tea there was a bacon and egg pie and a cake with
cherries in it. I was hungry too, and I ate without paying
much attention to what the others were saying. It was while
I was eating my cake, picking out the best of the cherries

and saving them till last, that I heard my aunt say : 'She's been asking questions again. I don't know what to say, I really don't.'

I looked up and caught the expression on my uncle's face. 'Not now, Bess,' he said. 'We'll talk about it later.'

Then he extracted the biggest of the cherries from his own slice of cake and laid it on my plate, saying : 'There you are. There's a nice big cherry for my little girl.'

I ate it to please him because his face was crinkled up in a smile, but there was no longer any sweetness in the cherry and when my aunt offered me another slice I shook my head. When tea was over bedtime was not far away, and bedtime meant the darkness and the dream.

I did not know how to bear it. I would rather run away, out into the night, down the lane past the cottage gardens, feeling my way by clinging to the wooden palings, right along to where there was a stile which led over on to a grassy path, and on one side of the path was a high thorn hedge and the other side was the river. I had walked with my uncle along the path and asked him where it led and he had replied : 'If you go to the left it leads to Oxford – that's where I go to work each day. But if you go to the right it goes on and on, ever so many miles, all the way to London. It's called the tow-path and it goes all along the river, some- times one side and sometimes the other, all the way to London town.'

I felt sure that my mother was in London and that if I was there too I would never have the dream again.

'You can look at your book for another ten minutes, Ruth,' said my aunt, 'and then it's time for bed.'

She picked up the tray with the dirty tea-things and clattered along the stone floor of the passage to the scullery. She made a surprising lot of noise for such a small person.

'Always got her nose in a book, Matthew,' I could hear her say. 'She doesn't seem to want to play like other children. I don't know what to do with her, I really don't.'

My uncle mumbled a reply but I could not hear the words. When he came back I was reading about King Arthur and the magic sword in the stone, my fingers clamped over my ears, shutting out everything else.

He came and sat in his big black armchair, poked at the fire, and rubbed his hands together. He asked me about the book and promised to get me down another one from the high shelf above the piano.

'And when you've finished them I'll find you some more,' he added. 'Miss Murry – the headmistress – has a great pile of books and she says we can borrow some if we keep them clean. And we'll play the piano too. It's years since I played the hymns but I can still pick out "God Save the King" and "All Things Bright and Beautiful" if I try. And when summer comes we'll ask Billy if we can borrow his boat and we'll row right down the river – down to the island where we used to pitch our tent when we were boys. I've got a picture of us somewhere, the three of us. Now where did I put that photograph album?'

He was feeling about in the cupboard in the wall at the side of the fireplace, just by the spot where the face had shot out of the wall in my dream. It came back now, the full horror of it, here in the warm bright room, with my dear uncle close by me, talking of his boyhood days, tales I loved to hear.

I got up from my stool and pulled at his arm.

'Uncle Matthew! Uncle Matthew!'

'Hullo, 'ullo, 'ullo.' He took me on his knee. 'What's up with my lassie? What's ailing my Ruthie?'

I wanted to cry but could not. It was always so terribly difficult to cry.

'My mummy – where is my mummy?' I asked.

'Oh, that's it, is it,' he said. His blue eyes opened very wide and he pursed up his mouth. 'Of course you want to know about your mummy. Every little girl wants to, even when she's got an old uncle and auntie who love her as much as we do.'

He hugged me and stroked my hair and I thought he would go on talking, but he said nothing for so long that I had to ask again : 'Where has she gone? Why has my mummy gone?'

'She's gone a long, long way away.'

After he had said this he fell silent again.

'Farther than London?' I prompted.

'Much, much farther than London. She's gone to Australia. On a big ship. It takes weeks and weeks to get there.'

'Will she write to me?' I asked.

'Yes,' he replied, 'but the letter has to come on the steamer too and it takes a long time, so you must be very patient, dear little Ruth, and try not to think about it too much every day.'

I was filled with a terrible desolation at these words. It was as bad as the terror of the dream.

'Why did she go?' I asked.

'Because she had no money after your daddy died and a lady said if she would go with her to Australia and do all her sewing and look after her, then she would pay your mummy a lot of money.'

He stopped again.

'But why didn't I go too?' I asked.

'It's such a long way,' said my uncle, 'such a very long journey for little girls, and besides, supposing you had gone too, what should I have done without my little Ruthie?'

His blue eyes opened very wide again and it seemed to me that I had to pretend to be satisfied in order to make him happy. So I said nothing more, and I went to bed shivering between the fear on the one side and the desolation on the other, like the prickly hedge and the deep water on the sides of the grassy path, and I longed more and more to go along that path, because it led to London, and from London I could get to Australia, where everything would be open and free, and where I could find my mother.

I slept for a while and then once again I woke in terror. It was in me and all around me, in the stories of knights and castles, in the grassy path that led to escape. It stifled me; I could not breathe, I could not cry out. Somehow or other I got out of bed and ran across the landing to the other room; I gripped one of the brass knobs at the foot of the bedstead and tried to speak. No sound came.

There were stirrings in the bed, a deep sigh, and an interrupted snore. I felt my way along the side of the bed, clutching at the counterpane. Still I could not speak.

'What — what's this — '

My uncle shook himself and sat up.

'What's the matter with her?' asked my aunt sleepily.

'I — I — ' It was like trying to pull water up from a deep well, this trying to speak. 'I keep thinking,' I managed at last. 'I keep seeing terrible things.'

My uncle put an arm round me.

'What do you see, lassie?' he asked. 'Tell your old uncle and he'll send it away.'

My aunt was getting out of bed. 'I'll heat up some milk,' she said, 'and don't you let her talk, Matthew. If she's been through a bad time like you say she has then it's best for her to forget it. And for us too. Now mind you don't encourage her to talk. We don't want to hear about any nasty things here, nothing nasty here.'

She left the room, repeating the phrase again and again.

'What's frightened you, Ruthie?' asked my uncle, lifting me up on to the bed beside him. 'Tell your old uncle, do.'

I cried a little then, at last, but still I could not speak. Words were such powerful and vivid things. They had magic in them, both good and bad. I read them on the page and they brought the whole of King Arthur's court into my mind. That was the good. But if I put the horror of the dream into words, how greatly might that increase its power. If I spoke of the head in the wall, it might take its revenge. And suppose it attacked my uncle and aunt too, so that they were struck helpless and could no longer care for me?

I clung to my uncle.

'Well, well,' he said, 'perhaps your auntie is right. Perhaps talking does no good. Never mind. Nothing shall hurt you here. You'll drink up your hot milk and then you'll stay with us till morning light. And it will all be forgot and tomorrow is Saturday and after dinner we'll wrap up very warm and go for a row in the boat. You'll like that, won't you?'

'Yes,' I replied, and then my aunt came back and I drank the milk, and she and my uncle each took a sip too, and they put me between them and I lay there pressed against the soft feathers of mattress and pillow, amidst the acid smell and creaky breathing of old people, feeling strange and out of place but no longer so afraid.

CHAPTER II

ONE DAY my uncle asked me if I would like to go to school.
I thought he meant that I should go with him on the bicycle
to Oxford and see the school-house and the gardens and the
young lady boarders. I thought this would be better than
going with my aunt to the village shop and hanging around
while she talked to Mrs Frost, and then coming back to feel
guilty if I read my book while she was scrubbing and
cooking, but not knowing how I could help her or what else
I should do; so I said yes, I should like very much to go to
school. There were daffodils and crocuses in the cottage
gardens now, and a shimmer of reddish-gold on the willow-
trees that hung over the water round my uncle's little island.

'And can I see the new rock garden,' I asked, 'and the
bird bath?'

He looked puzzled, although he had been talking only a
few minutes previously about the work he had been doing
on them. Then he said: 'Of course you shall. In the holidays perhaps. I'm sure Miss Murry won't mind if I take
you along one day. But I meant, to go properly to school.
Wouldn't you like to go and play with all the other little
girls and boys in the village?'

He looked at me pleadingly and I said 'Yes, Uncle' very
quietly, because I was so very disappointed. To go with him
into the town would have been a step towards the big open
world where I would be free to look for my mother; but
to go to the village school here in Littleford meant going
with the twins in the cottage next door. They were a couple
of stupid-looking, red-faced children who stood staring at

me over the fence whenever I went into the garden. The
boy would take his thumb out of his mouth for long enough
to say : 'Where's your mummy?' And then he would put
it back in again and that was all the conversation we ever
had.

I dreaded the thought of the village school but I could
not explain this to my uncle. It was like all the other fears
– to talk about it might make it worse, just as to show how
disappointed I was would mean feeling it all the more
keenly. It was at this moment that I made a little vow to
myself, or rather two little vows : never look forward to
anything or hope for anything, never show that you care.
I worked it out that this was the way to stop being hurt
and disappointed, and I resolved that when the postman
knocked at the cottage door I would no longer run to my
aunt and ask her if there was a letter for me. I would
pretend I didn't expect one, and perhaps, I thought, if I
pretended well enough, perhaps one day there would be one
after all.

So I made no protest when my aunt told me to fetch my
best hair ribbon because we were going to see the teacher,
and she tied my plaits very tight and pulled my coat on with
a jerk, because my hands were shaking so much that I could
not find the armholes for myself.

There was an iron railing and a gate into a hard asphalt
yard that was crowded with girls and boys. There seemed
to be nothing but red faces and open mouths shouting and
screaming. It was like the dream and I could scarcely move.
My aunt pulled me along. We went into a big room with
long pointed windows like a church. There was a big round
black stove in the middle of one wall and somebody was
bending over it, raking out the ashes. As we came nearer
she straightened up and became taller and taller and taller.

She seemed to be twice the height of my aunt and very thin. And she was all grey – dark grey clothes, light grey hair, and a big grey smudge on her nose where she had been bending over the stove.

'Rotten old thing,' she said, taking a handkerchief from a pocket and wiping her hands on it. 'Sometimes I think I'd sell my soul for a nice electric fire.'

I had taken hold of my aunt's hand, and perhaps it was something about the way it stiffened in my grasp that told me Aunt Bessie did not like the teacher.

'I hope we're not inconveniencing you,' she said in the sort of voice she used to my uncle when she was going to complain about something, 'but I thought as it was play-time – '

'No, no, of course not,' said the teacher. She had a low clear voice that reminded me of something. It seemed to be linked up with words on the pages of a book with beautiful pictures and there was a feeling of safety and comfort about it.

'So this is Ruth,' she said, holding out a hand to me. 'Thank you for bringing her along, Mrs Baines. Would you like to see where she is going to sit?'

We went to the far end of the room and stopped at one of the desks in the front row.

'These are for the younger ones,' said the teacher. 'Miss Foster looks after them a lot of the time, but I take them for arithmetic. Do you like arithmetic, Ruth?'

She turned to me and I wanted to reply but my aunt jumped in before I could speak.

'Oh, she's always doing sums, doing sums for fun, she says. Did you ever hear of such a child? And reading! You can't get her to take her nose out of a book.'

'So you like reading, do you, Ruth,' said the teacher,

turning to me again. 'That's very good. Most of the children this end of the room are only just learning. Perhaps you'll be able to help some of them. We don't often have the pleasure of taking in a new pupil who can read already.'

The lovely voice, the kind smiling face such a long way above me, the feeling of openness in the long room with the high windows, so different from the crowded little cottage, all these joined together to produce an extraordinary effect on me, like one of the daffodil buds bursting out in the sunshine.

'My mummy taught me!' I cried at the top of my voice. 'My mummy taught me!'

There was silence in the room for a moment or two and the screams from the playground outside sounded very loud.

'Then you will have been well taught,' said the teacher at last, 'and I'm sure you will show us how well she taught you.'

My aunt began to bustle and to talk of all the things she had got to do and how she mustn't waste any more time. The teacher took my hand.

'I'll show you where you hang your coat and then we'll go and meet Miss Foster,' she said.

It was like a miracle, good magic instead of bad. It all came from pretending I wasn't disappointed, pretending I did not care. Instead of dreading to go to school, I longed to go. It was an escape, a step along the path towards finding my mother. I no longer cared when the stupid twins next door came up and asked me where my mummy was.

'She's gone away to make a lot of money,' I replied.

Of course they wanted to know where.

'A long way away, somewhere you wouldn't know about,' I said quite unkindly.

I made the same sort of answer to others who asked me

B

the same question. 'She's very clever,' I said. 'She taught me to read and write and do sums and now she has gone away to make a lot of money. When she comes back we shall be very rich and have a big house by the river with a boathouse and a gardener to look after the flowers.'

They could all see that I could read and write and do sums, and I think this inclined them to believe the rest of what I said too, so I was not troubled very much. Only one little boy asked me where my daddy was.

'He was killed in the trenches in the Great War,' I said instantly.

They understood this. A lot of them had had fathers killed in the Great War too. One day when we were playing hopscotch, which I enjoyed because the lines and figures on the asphalt were a sort of magic and I had command over it, the same little boy pushed me aside and said : 'We don't want you. Teacher's pet.'

They all took up the words in a chorus : 'Teacher's pet, teacher's pet,' and made faces at me.

'If you won't let me play I won't do your sums for you any more!' I cried.

It worked like magic. They sulked and muttered but they let me play and I won the game. When we did sums in class I would work out mine very quickly and write the answers in big figures in my exercise book, which I then held propped up on my desk so that the girl at the desk behind could see what I had written. She would then do the same, and in this way the answer went all round the class. Miss Greenfield – that was the tall teacher's name – didn't realize at first what was happening.

'Good, good, very good indeed. Well done, class,' she said, as one child after another produced the correct answer.

But after a while she became suspicious, and when she was writing up the next sum for us on the blackboard she suddenly turned round as if she was playing a game of grandmother's steps and caught Minnie, who sat next to me, in the very act of waving her exercise book in the air above her head. She didn't say anything then, but she put a very difficult sum on the board and I made a mistake in the multiplication, and all the rest of the class had the wrong answer too. Then she said, shaking her head : 'It's very odd, very odd indeed, to find so many people putting seven instead of eight. Sevens must be catching, like measles.'

One or two of the boys gave a little titter, and Miss Greenfield didn't tell them to be quiet, but they very soon stopped because although nothing was said, of course we all knew that she knew. After that we were more careful about holding up the books and I tried to show some of the class how to do the sums themselves and was very pleased when Minnie cried : 'Oh, I see !'

And she wriggled along the seat of the desk when Miss Greenfield had gone to the other end of the room, and put an arm round my neck and kissed me, all because I had shown her how to carry one when you added six and six together. Here was more magic indeed. Knowing things could make people love you, and I formed a new resolve to add to the others : never let it be seen that you don't know.

After that I had a real friend of my very own – Minnie, who thought I knew everything. She came to visit us in the cottage and my aunt liked her because she was pretty and clean and had a fair curly head and laughed a lot.

'Oh dear,' Aunt Bessie would sigh as she struggled with my heavy dark red hair, 'if only it was like Minnie's.'

I didn't mind. I rather liked having hair that was different. I felt as if I held a great weight of secrets inside me, as if I knew all sorts of things that gave me power over other people. I was pretending, but they did not know I was. It was like having a great invisible shield protecting me.

CHAPTER III

AT FIRST I thought of sharing the secret with Miss Greenfield. She was kind and I loved to hear her voice. But although she said again and again, 'You will always come and tell me, Ruth, won't you, if ever anything is troubling you,' yet I could never quite bring myself to do it.

Once there was a great fight going on outside the school gate between the bulldog from the village shop and a big fierce black dog that had suddenly appeared and seemed to have no owner, and we were all afraid to go out of the playground. But Miss Greenfield came out and got them apart and held them while we all ran home, so I knew she was very brave. I didn't think she would be frightened, as my aunt was frightened, if I tried to talk to her about my mummy, but I could not be quite sure so it seemed safer to say nothing. When I had the dream, though, and woke up sick and shivering, full of the feeling of the head jumping out at me, I would cling tight to the sheets and say: 'Go away, I'll tell Miss Greenfield about you.'

It helped a little and I was not so afraid during the time I went to Miss Greenfield's school. She taught me a lot and was delighted that I learned so quickly and one day she said that she was going to talk to my uncle about plans for my further education after I reached the top of the school.

'Of course you'll be here for some years yet, Ruth,' she said, 'but we ought to be thinking about it now because if you are going on to be a scholar then you ought to be starting Latin.' And a moment later she added, as much to herself as to me : 'It's the first time I've had the pleasure of teaching a child who is university material since I came to Littleford.'

I didn't fully understand her, but I was delighted at the prospect of learning Latin. As things turned out, however, I never reached the top of the school, and it all came about because of the terrible secret that I carried about with me.

It was a bright, long, happy summer day, and Uncle Matthew and Minnie's father had taken us all the way up the river to Oxford and back. I sat with Minnie in the bows of the boat, on a red cushion, and leaned over the side so that I could trail my fingers in the water and feel myself to be on the move. My uncle had his back to us, as he was rowing, and Minnie's father sat in the stern with the steering-ropes. They kept calling our attention to things on the bank :

'Look, girls, there's the long white bridges and the new swimming-pool – there's the first of the college barges – – here's the River Cherwell. That's an eight – a college eight – see how fast it goes.'

I left it to Minnie to bounce about and say 'Oh yes,' and 'What's that, Dad?' I was in a daydream of escape, lulled by lapping water, drowsy from the heat and glare of the sun. Even when we pulled in to the towpath because Minnie had seen an ice-cream boy on a bicycle, I still did not rouse myself, but licked at my cone in a lazy way and took the first opportunity, when nobody was looking in my direction, to drop the rest of it in the water. I never liked ice-cream, but since people thought they were giving you a treat by buying you one it seemed unkind to refuse.

So we came back home, and my Aunt Bessie and Minnie's mother had made us an enormous tea. The table was pulled out from the wall so that we could all sit round it and the room felt very crowded. Minnie chattered a lot and her mother and father laughed loudly at everything she said. I was not exactly jealous, because she was rather a silly little girl and they were rather silly people, but there was a blackness inside me that swelled and swelled until it blotted out all the memory of the bright sky and the lapping water and the chunky movement of the rowing-boat. There was no fear; just nothing, and I looked round the table at the grinning red faces and described them in my mind and felt that I had power over them, power to destroy them with my words.

After tea Minnie and I were sent to play in the back garden while the others washed up.

'What shall we do?' I asked. 'Shall we climb the apple-tree?'

Minnie refused. 'It would spoil my dress,' she said, 'and Mummy wouldn't like it,' and catching sight of the twins in the garden next door she ran over and pressed herself against the fence and I heard her say: 'I've been in a boat all the way to Oxford. I saw the bridge and I had an ice.'

I didn't hear what the twins replied. The blackness inside me had turned to a terrible rage. I hated Minnie, hated the twins. I wanted to hit them, kick them, tear at their fat pink faces with my finger-nails. I could not bear to see them; I could not bear anyone to see me. I ran to the back door of the cottage and crept behind the bushes that grew under the scullery window. There was just room for me to crouch between the white-washed wall and the branches which drooped close to the ground, and nobody could see me there. I heard Minnie's voice as if it were a very long way off, and the twins' voices, and the slight rustle of the leaves of the bushes in the breeze, and the splashing of water running from the scullery sink into the drain by the back door.

They must be still washing up, I thought, and then I heard their voices too. A thin, complaining little voice that must have belonged to my aunt, though it sounded different from when you could see her too, and a strange voice that must have been Minnie's mother's, but I didn't recognize it because I had never noticed what sort of voice she had; I had only thought of her as a grinning face with fair hair.

'What a burden it must be to you,' this voice was saying. 'I think it's very good of you to have her, I do really.'

Then came the chinky noise of cups and plates being moved.

'Oh dear, yes,' said my aunt with one of her big sighs. 'A most dreadful burden it is indeed. But Matthew would do it. He's so soft, he'd give his last penny to the first scrounger who told him a hard luck tale. And when the lady told him about this trouble of one of her old pupils who she was so fond of, and how she was looking for somewhere that the child could be brought up right away from it all and where nobody knew anything about it, well in he jumps, both feet first, and says "*We'll* take her." "*We'll* take her," he says, not even thinking to ask me! And who is to have all the work and worry of it, I'd like to know – that's what I said when he came home that night – who is to have all the work and all the worry!'

The thin voice, which had become shriller and shriller, now ceased. Who is she talking about, I wondered dully; I never knew anything about this child. Then the strange voice spoke again:

'Well, I think it's very good of you, I really do. It's not
even as if you're any relation. And not even knowing who
the father was. Why, he might have been anything – a
criminal maybe!'

The voice stopped with a gasp and I could picture the
big face with its mouth wide open, staring stupidly.

'*He* knows,' said the shrill voice. 'He says he doesn't but
I know he does. He knows and he won't tell me because
he knows I'd never have had anything to do with the child
if I knew. So it must be something very dreadful, very
dreadful.'

She stopped suddenly and I heard the sound of breaking
china.

'Now look what you've made me do, Matthew,' she
scolded, 'creeping in like that! Mother's best tea service and
never a piece missing until this very day . . .'

The complaining voice went on and on and every now
and then my uncle murmured something but I did not hear
the words. I lay on the soft cool earth underneath the bush,
with my back pressed up against the wall of the cottage,
and my hands felt out for one of the low branches. There
was a piece of bark peeling off and I picked and pulled at
it as if it was a scab that had formed over a wound. It came
away, leaving other loose flaps of bark, and I pulled at
them too, until several inches of the branch were exposed.
It looked pale, naked, defenceless. It seemed to have taken
on a life of its own and to be crying out to me in pain :
don't do it, I am too weak, I am not ready yet. Don't take
away my protection. I held my hands tight round the pale
stick of wood. It was as if I could feel the sap running
through it, its life blood, and I wished I could replace its
torn covering and make it once again warm and safe.
I think I cried a little then : poor branch, poor branch.

'Ruth!'

I heard my uncle's voice very near. He was standing at the back door of the cottage. By peeping between the branches I could just see his feet.

'Ruth!' he cried again, and then to himself in a low voice: 'Where can the child have got to? Pray heaven she did not hear.'

I could not call out to tell him where I was. It was not because I wanted him to worry about me, for I loved him and hated it when his wife scolded him; but I felt dirty and ashamed, as if I was not fit to be seen, and it was nothing to do with my dress being smudged and crumpled from my lying on the ground.

'Minnie,' he cried, 'where is Ruth? I thought you two were playing.'

I put my hands over my ears. I could not bear to hear Minnie's reply. I hated her too much, hated her red-faced mother, hated her stupid father with his loud laugh, hated my Aunt Bessie whom I dimly understood was not my aunt at all. It was like molten steel pouring through me, all this hatred, giving me strength, taking away the dirt and the shame and the nakedness. The words of hatred came flooding into my mind, hurting stabbing words that seemed to put them all at my mercy.

I felt movement in the branches of the bush and my heart seemed to stop. I took my hands from my ears and peeped out. My uncle brushed past only a couple of feet from where I lay, muttering anxiously to himself.

'In the shed maybe. Or did she creep upstairs with a book?'

Then he called in a louder voice: 'Come along, Minnie. Come and help look for Ruth.'

Again the branches moved as he tramped past me and I

heard the loud voice of the mother of the twins next door calling them in. Then there was silence save for the birds and the faint rustle of leaves. The garden was empty; it was my one chance to find a new hiding-place, and I must move quickly, for when they had searched the house and shed in vain they would surely think of the bushes. I wriggled along under the back wall of the cottage until I reached the fence and then I ran the few yards to the bottom of the garden and flung myself down in the long grass around the apple-tree.

There was no sign of pursuit. Hatred turned to contempt. The fools, I thought, they can't even find me. I was almost beginning to enjoy myself. It was I who had the secret now.

I dragged myself along the grass to where there was a gap in the hedge at the bottom of the garden, crawled through, and rolled about in the long grass on the other side. There were buttercups and moon-daisies and the long red-brown knobbly stalks of dock. I clutched at them and gathered a little bunch, thinking of Uncle Matthew. He had taught me their names; he had said that wild flowers were just as precious as those grown in a garden. Then I stood up and looked across the field. The black and white cows were in the far corner, near the river. The shadows were longer now, the sky a paler blue, but it was still very warm and sparkling and as I walked along by the hedge, adding to my bunch whenever I saw a fine crisp daisy or a glistening buttercup, all the hatred and contempt drained away, and Aunt Bessie and Minnie and her parents with their fat faces and stupid talk were like a fading dream. And I myself was free, a part of the bright meadow and the pearly sky, along with the birds and the cows and the insects that buzzed around the flowers that I held in my hand.

When I came to the end of the field I climbed over the

gate and set off along the path by the river, still holding my now wilting flowers but feeling a little quickening of excitement now that I was no longer in the dreamy meadow but was once more among people, with a great stretch of the wide free world spread out before me. I heard the splash of oars and the cheerful cries of the people in the boats; and I felt the swish of their skirts near my face as a group of tall, laughing girls in bright summer frocks came past me on the narrow path. They had rolled-up towels under their arms and were going to the bathing-pool. I stopped to watch a boy fishing and asked him, very boldly, whether he had caught anything. He showed me his jam-jar full of tiddlers and said he was doing much better than his brother, who was fishing farther up the river.

'Oh,' I said, 'I'll go and find him.'

'Tell him I've caught thirteen!' shouted the boy after me.

But I made no attempt to find the brother. The thought that these two little boys had got each other, and more of them too perhaps at home, filled me with a sudden black envy that took all the brightness from the sky and I sat down on the bank and dangled my feet over the side and stared at the water. It was brown and muddy, here by the bank, and the passing boats kept sending along ripples that disturbed the surface, but I could still make out my reflection – a blurred, wavering image. She stared back at me, this Ruth who lived in another world, a world of sky and water. The more I looked the more she seemed to call to me. If I could join her there, I thought, join her in the sky and water, escape from everything else for ever and ever, then all my troubles would be at an end. My hands gripped the tufts of grass at my side as I leaned forward to get a better view. I felt myself slipping; the river-Ruth moved towards me.

'I'm coming!' I cried.

At the very moment that I began to let the grass slip away under my fingers I felt a sharp tug at the back of my dress. Hands came under my arms and pulled me up and stood me on the path.

'That's a silly place to sit,' said a deep voice.

I was staring down at some dusty brown shoes and some grey flannel trouser legs. I looked up and felt so giddy that I nearly fell. The hands that had pulled me up caught hold of me again and the tall thin man crouched down in front of me so that his face with the big horn-rimmed spectacles was near to my own.

'Who d'you belong to?' he asked. 'Where's your mother? I'm sure she doesn't want you falling into the river.'

To my great shame I found I was crying. Usually I found it very difficult to cry, but now, once having started, I found it just as hard to stop.

'School . . . Miss Murry . . . at school,' I said between sobs.

'School? Miss Murry?' he repeated to himself in a puzzled way. And then, with a switch to the special sort of voice that people use for talking to children, he went on : 'Are you on a school outing?'

I nodded vigorously and continued to sob.

'Where are all the others? Which way did they go? D'you think you could try and tell me so that I can help you find them?'

I thought for a moment under cover of my crying. I had not really meant to mislead him, but I was genuinely confused in my mind and did not know how to explain. But it occurred to me now that if I told him I had run away from Uncle Matthew's cottage he would insist on taking me back there, and I would have to see Auntie Bessie, whom I hated so much. So I pointed my hand in the direction of the bridge with the three stone arches, which was not very far distant now, since I had walked a long way from Littleford.

The man straightened up and took hold of my hand. 'We'll try and catch them up, shall we?' he said. 'They can't have gone very far and they'll soon notice that you are missing and will turn back for you. What did you say the name of your teacher was?'

'Miss Greenfield,' I said without thinking, and then, before he could speak, I corrected myself. 'I mean Miss Murry. I forgot.'

He was a nice, kind man but he was as stupid as grown-ups always were. He saw that I was lost and tired and rather frightened, but he didn't imagine that I could still be cunning.

'Murry, Murry,' he said again in the talking-to-himself voice. 'Girls' boarding-school? It seems to strike a chord somewhere. Oh yes. Headmistress of St Margaret's. I wonder if that could be the one? I wouldn't have expected her to take the children out herself, and it's strange that they should come down to this end of the town for their walks and one would have thought they would be in uniform. But perhaps with the very young ones and at the weekend . . .'

His voice tailed away but he kept hold of my hand and we walked along. I felt safe and happy with him and was very glad now that I had not fallen into the river. When we reached the bridge he said: 'It doesn't look as if we are going to catch them up. Are you quite sure they were not going farther along the towpath?'

I began to cry again, louder this time because I was putting it on.

'Don't know,' I said hopelessly. 'I want to go home.'

'Perhaps I'd better take you straight back to the school,' said the man in a mixed sort of voice, half to me and half to himself. 'I live up that way so it's simple enough. Never knew she took quite such young boarders – she'll be dreadfully worried if she can't find you on the towpath – perhaps after all we'd better turn back and try to find the rest of the party.'

'I'm so tired,' I cried in a great wail.

'All right, child. What's your name? Ruth. All right then, Ruth, we'll get straight on a bus and take you home.'

In the bus I had to keep pretending to cry again because he would ask me questions about the school and about myself, and although I could easily have made up a story, I didn't want to do so now. All I wanted was to meet Miss Murry and ask her where I could find my mother, because I was quite sure that she would know. She had sent me to live with Uncle Matthew – that much I had understood from my overhearing – and therefore she must know where I had lived before. I pictured her as tall and grey and clever, like Miss Greenfield, and she must be kind, because Uncle Matthew liked her so much. But I didn't want anything to go wrong now, so I thought it safest to say nothing at all to this strange man who was going to take me to Miss Murry's school.

The bus was crowded inside, so we had to climb the outside staircase and sit in the open air on one of the slatted seats. It was the first time I could remember having been on a bus, and it was a great pity to have to keep sobbing and rubbing my eyes when I was longing to peer over the side and look at everything that was going on in the busy streets of Oxford. Once I did forget myself. We came to a great wide street with old grey buildings and trees down either side.

'What's it called?' I asked.

'St Giles,' replied the man. 'He was patron saint of beggars. Every year at the beginning of September they have a fair here – coconut shies and roundabouts and all. And the traffic is diverted round the back streets.'

'Oh what fun!' I cried without thinking.

'It depends on your taste in amusement,' he said in a grown-up way, and then he spoke in the puzzled voice again :

'You must have been this way before. I'd have thought you would have known this was St Giles.'

I looked up at him, and instead of the sweet old blue eyes of Uncle Matthew, I saw dark brown eyes that seemed to know everything and that could see through my pretence; the big spectacles only made them look all the wiser.

I thought of saying that I had forgotten, and then I thought of pretending to cry again, but in the end it seemed best to do neither. So I just asked about St Giles, because surely I could not be expected to know about him, and he told me a story and made it sound so interesting that I began to wish I could stay with him for a long time.

CHAPTER IV

WE GOT off the bus and turned into a leafy side road with high brick walls and tall trees sheltering big yellow-grey houses that looked like castles. We went through the gates of one of these and walked up to the great front door. The strange man pulled the bell and now for the first time I felt apprehensive.

'Will she be very angry?' I asked, clinging to his hand.

'I don't see why she should be, Ruth,' he replied. 'It was her fault as much as yours that you got detached from the rest of the party. I expect she'll be so relieved to see you that she won't be angry at all.'

He spoke in an ordinary, friendly voice now, such as grown-ups use to each other, and not in the special voice for children. I began to like him more and more and wished I had not played him up with my crying and caused him all this trouble. The bell was answered by a little person in a blue overall who looked rather like my Aunt Bessie.

'Miss Murry?' she said. 'Who shall I say it is, sir?'

I didn't hear his reply. I was very confused and troubled now. We were in a high hall, with a great polished staircase in front and lots of closed doors on every side. We must have gone through one of them because suddenly, as in a dream, we were in a room with high windows looking out on to a tennis court where people were playing. There were shelves and shelves of books and some armchairs and a desk where a lady was sitting. On the desk was a great bowl of roses, crimson and pink. Their scent filled the room and stirred something in me that took away the fearfulness. The roses and the armchairs and the space and light and the lovely garden beyond – I could not exactly remember having been in a room like this before and yet at the same time it did not feel completely strange. And the more I looked the less strange it seemed, and it seemed to be linked up with my learning to read, spelling out the words one by one in the book with the blue cover and the picture of the Roman soldier standing on the bridge with his sword drawn, defending his city against all the invaders crowding in. I had struggled with the word 'sword'; it didn't sound right from the letters. And a kind voice had explained:

'You don't sound the "w", dear . . .'

It had been in a room like this. And someone had cared for me. I stared and stared. I had come home, and everything else that I could remember in my life mattered no more than a dream.

The lady got up from the desk and came towards us. She wasn't a bit like Miss Greenfield. Her hair was dark and thick and smooth, done up in a plait wound round her head. Her eyes were dark and her face was pale. It was linked up with the room and the roses and it seemed to be a face I knew. I let go of the strange man's hand and ran towards her.

'Miss – Miss –' There was a name that I ought to be saying but I could not remember it.

'Miss –' I cried again, and then, as if my heart itself was speaking and not my lips at all, I burst out with a loud cry of 'Mummy!'

'This is Miss Murry, Ruth,' corrected the deep voice of the strange man.

'I know,' I said quickly, afraid that they might laugh at my silly mistake. 'I know it's Miss Murry.'

But actually I had been quite confused for a moment or two and even now I was not quite sure which of the two had taught me to read, the lady or my own mother.

'Well,' said the strange man, 'now that I've delivered her safely, I think I'd better be going.'

'It's very kind of you, Professor West,' said the lady. 'I won't keep you a moment, but if you could just tell me how and where you found her.'

I was holding tight to the hem of her thin jacket, and she put an arm round me. I didn't hear what the man said. I was still very muddled and afraid of saying something stupid in my confusion, but at the same time I felt

c

absolutely safe, as if everything was going to be put right for ever. I tried not to think how wonderful it was, though, because I was afraid the spell might be broken. Pretend not to care, pretend it doesn't matter, I kept repeating to myself, and then perhaps it will all last a little longer.

The strange man left the room, saying : 'Goodbye, Ruth, I expect we shall meet again,' and when he had gone I began to talk straight away, for fear that the lady would say something that I didn't want to hear.

'I wanted to see the garden,' I said. 'Uncle Matthew told me how lovely the roses were.' I buried my face in the bowl and sniffed. 'M'm. I like the red ones best, don't you?'

She seemed to consider for a moment before replying, and then she said : 'Yes. They are my favourites too. We'll go and pick a few more, shall we?'

She was smoothing my hair and brushing my dress as she spoke and for the first time since running away I realized that I was very dirty and untidy from scrambling through hedges and crawling along the grass and I felt ashamed.

'That'll do for the moment,' she said. 'What a nuisance these white frocks are when you want to go tree-climbing. If I had my way I would put you into khaki shorts – the whole lot of you – boys and girls alike. And myself too. But I can't do that because I'm headmistress of a school and I have to be ladylike because the parents expect it. Now, Ruth, that's made you more or less presentable. You'd better inspect me and see if I will do. The girls' parents tend to wander round the place on a Saturday evening, you see, after coming to visit the boarders and taking them out to tea. So you never know who you are going to run into.'

She turned round and asked: 'Do I look all right?'

'Yes,' I said, 'you look fine.'

'Good. Then we'll go and walk round the garden.'

It was like paradise on this lovely summer evening, and the longer I was in it the less could I believe that I would ever be sent away again.

'There's the new rock garden, your uncle's pride and joy,' she said.

And then she suddenly left my side and dashed away to where a girl somewhat bigger than myself was holding a little black cat round the neck, crushing it down to the grass and ignoring its writhings and pitiful mewings.

'Now, Julie,' said Miss Murry sharply, 'you are not to tease the kitten. I shall give it away if you won't learn to play with it properly.'

The girl got up and stood with her head hanging shame-facedly, her arms turning together behind her back. The cat gave a loud squeal and shot up a tree.

'This is Ruth,' said Miss Murry. 'She may be coming here as a boarder next term.'

'Hullo,' said Julie, peering sideways at me suspiciously.

'Hullo,' I said, disliking her.

'It's past your bedtime, anyway,' said Miss Murry to the girl. 'Run off and find Rosemary and go and get your milk.'

When Julie had gone she turned to me and said: 'They are our two youngest boarders. It's very hard to have to go to bed on a bright summer evening when the older girls are still in the garden, so I am not too hard on them if they are a little late.'

I did not know what to say. It was as if a great shadow had suddenly come up and darkened the evening. It was past my bedtime too and I was in a strange place among strangers and yet my own home was no longer my home. But she had told Julie I was to come as a boarder. Did she really mean it?

'We'll go round to the front and look at the dahlias,' said Miss Murry, 'although of course they are scarcely in bud yet. And then you will have seen it all.'

But as we came round the side of the school-house, two girls came rushing up. They were some years older than myself and they wore the cream-coloured school hats and blue cotton frocks. Behind them came a tall man in a light grey suit and a woman in a big floppy hat and a very pretty white dress.

'Here we are, Miss Murry,' she cried gaily. 'We've had a lovely afternoon on the river and we're returning them both safe and sound.'

Miss Murry pressed my shoulder and said quietly: 'Excuse me a minute, Ruth. I shan't be long. You run off and look at some more of the flowers, but don't go too far.'

I ran to a big tree near the front gate and stood behind it, out of sight of the others. The shadow was right inside me now and I felt as if I was choking. I hated the tall man and the beautiful lady and the two great girls, and I hated Miss Murry for sending me away. It was as bad as it had been when I lay behind the bushes and listened to Aunt Bessie and Minnie's mother talking.

I climbed up the grassy slope behind the tree and looked over the wall into the road. A man on a bicycle was riding slowly along and he got off at the gate of the school. Had he looked up he would have seen me only a few feet away, but he kept his eyes on the ground and I could not see his face. It was the old brown cap and the crooked old fingers clutching the gate-post that told me it was Uncle Matthew.

He propped his bike up against the gate-post and walked

to where Miss Murry was still talking to the parents. He must have said something to her for she turned round and greeted him in a clear voice.

'Oh, Mr Baines, I am so glad you have come. I was hoping you might guess she had found her way here and that you would come in search of her.'

The words came at me like a blow. She was going to send me back. I could not bear it. I loved Uncle Matthew but I could not go back to Aunt Bessie who didn't want me, away from this place that held memories of home. I looked around for a way to escape. If I came down the grassy slope and ran through the gate they would see me and give chase. Any moment now they would start looking for me. In a blind panic I scrambled to the top of the slope and climbed on to the wall and sat there with my legs dangling over the pavement. It looked very far away and I couldn't see any sort of foothold. I twisted round and let myself down so that I hung against the wall with my fingers gripping the bricks at the top. My feet were still quite a distance from the ground but there was no going back now. My arms became weaker and weaker, my fingers were slipping on the bricks. I let go and I seemed to be falling for a very long time, as in a bad dream, and then something terribly hard came up and hit my legs and then it hit my head and then everything was dark and still.

CHAPTER V

I HAD slight concussion and had broken a leg and they put me in hospital and Uncle Matthew and Miss Murry came to see me. Aunt Bessie didn't come.

'She sends her love,' said Uncle Matthew, 'and she's going to make you a cake.'

I said nothing; I was too tired to pretend. But in spite of the pain in my head and leg I was happy in the hospital because I felt safe there. At night was the best, when the lights were turned out except for the one where nurse sat. She had a kind face and I could see it from where I lay. I didn't hate anyone there and I had no bad dreams. But I did remember something. I had been in hospital before. No one had ever told me this, but I recognized the feel and the smell of it. And I reasoned it out, step by step, as I used to work out the arithmetic problems that Miss Greenfield set me. I had been in hospital before, but nobody talked about it. Therefore it must have been connected with other things that had happened to me and were never talked about. Therefore it must have had something to do with my mother.

I said nothing about my discovery, not even to Miss Murry when she brought me a chess set and showed me the moves and I loved her for it. There was a little book with puzzles to work out and when I managed to get one right I felt strong and free and afraid of nothing, as I felt sometimes when I was reading, and as I had felt when I climbed through the hedge into the field at the end of Uncle Matthew's garden.

But he was not my uncle at all. He was gardener and handyman at Miss Murry's school, and nothing at all to do with me except that he had taken me to his cottage and given me a home when Miss Murry was at her wits' end what to do with me. And she wasn't really anything to do with me either, except that my mother had been at her school and had been very clever and Miss Murry had been very fond of her This much I had understood from my overhearing; and to it I could add from my own dim recollection the facts that I had sat in a room like Miss Murry's room, learning to read, and that I had been in hospital. So I could take for myself one more step towards the solution : my home – if I had ever had a home – must have been very different from Uncle Matthew's little cottage, because the girls at Miss Murry's school were not like Minnie and the other children at Miss Greenfield's. They had parents like the two I had seen in the garden; they had homes like Miss Murry's school-house, and my home must have been like that.

When I came to this conclusion I felt quite excited, because it made me feel like a princess in disguise, and it made me love Uncle Matthew all the more, as if he were the woodcutter in the fairy tale who had rescued me from the wicked godmother. But who the wicked godmother was I didn't yet know, although it seemed to me that she must be connected with the face in the dream.

The hospital days went by like the sure, steady ticking of a great clock, and I kept all these thoughts to myself.

One day, when I had managed to walk right down a long corridor and back with very little pain in my leg, the kind nurse said : 'You're getting on famously. We'll be saying goodbye to you soon.'

Of course I knew I should have to leave the hospital some time, but it had seemed a long way off. I stumbled and nearly fell. The nurse picked me up.

'There's no need for you to worry, darling. Why, what a silly I am! Of course nobody's told you.'

She panted and puffed. 'Heavens! What a weight you are! What a big girl you are growing into!'

She dumped me into my bed and arranged the bed-clothes.

'Nobody told me what?' I said. I had resolved never to
ask anything, but at this moment I was too shocked to
keep to my resolve.

The nurse pulled me up against the pillows.

'They'll be along soon and they'll tell you all about it,'
she said. 'It's all been arranged. You're going to ever such
a lovely home. But I'm not supposed to mention it, because
they wanted to tell you themselves. It's to be a lovely
surprise. So you'll pretend you don't know, just to please
me, won't you, darling?'

Of course I promised to pretend. My mind was already
busy on this new scrap of information, trying to fit it into
the pattern I had made. A lovely home. That couldn't be
the cottage in Littleford, because nobody could call that a
lovely home, and in any case nurse would have said 'to
Uncle Matthew's' if I had been going back there. She didn't
know that I knew he was not my uncle.

A lovely home. They were beautiful words and I couldn't
help but dream over them. But of course it's only a story,
I kept saying to myself; don't expect anything, then you
won't be disappointed. This time it worked a miracle. The
not expecting anything, I mean. The lovely home turned
out to be Miss Murry's own home, where she spent the
school holidays and many week-ends, and where her old
father lived all the time. It was a big house on the riverside, with lawns sloping down to the water's edge and a
boathouse with an arched roof that reminded me of a
church.

I recognized it all, I knew it well. We came into Miss
Murry's sitting-room, which was a big room rather like her
study at school except that it had a bay window overlooking
the river, and I knew instantly that it had been here, and

not in the study, that I had learned to read. But I didn't
let on as yet.

'What a lovely room!' I cried. 'May I sit in here?'

'Of course,' she said, 'but since the weather is so fine
we are going to put a chair out for you on the lawn.'

That was where I was sitting when Uncle Matthew first
bicycled over to see me. The house, which was called Rivermead, was only a few miles downstream from Littleford
village.

'Hullo, Ruthie,' he said, sitting down on the grass at my
side. 'Got a word for your poor old uncle now you're such
a grand lady?'

So we are still pretending that he is my uncle, I said to
myself, and for a moment I felt impatient and almost angry
with him. But his blue eyes looked at me as longingly as an
old dog's, and I leaned over and hugged him.

'You're in clover, aren't you?' he said. 'Do you like being
here?'

He sounded rather sad, but this was something I could
not pretend about.

'I love it,' I replied, and then hastily added: 'And I love
seeing you too.'

He brightened up then and I knew I ought to say that
I wished I could see Aunt Bessie, but this was another lie
I could not tell. I could scarcely remember what she looked
like, so little did she now matter in my life.

'Herbaceous border's coming along nicely,' he said,
looking around him, and there was something of proud
satisfaction in the way he spoke that told me at once that
he had planted it himself. Of course, I thought, he works
as gardener here at Miss Murry's home as well as at the
school, but that is another of the things I am not supposed

to know. Again I felt a little stab of anger mixed with contempt, but still I didn't show that I had remembered anything. I was biding my time. I guessed that Miss Murry was going to tell me something about my mother and I wanted to find out all I could for myself first so that I could check whether she was telling the truth. I had grown to love her and I believed that she cared for me but I still did not quite trust her. I asked no questions; I hoped she would say nothing until I had pieced some more scraps together, for I wanted to be able to stop her quickly if she started trying to tell me a lie. There must be plenty of clues here at Rivermead if I could but find them, but neither she nor Uncle Matthew nor the housekeeper, Mrs Winter, must know what I was searching for. In this they were all my enemies.

But old Mr Murry was my friend. He was very grey and frail and he didn't get up till the afternoons, when he sat in a big chair with a rug over his legs, gripping the arms and staring about him with faded blue eyes. I don't think he could see very well but he could hear everything and although Miss Murry had told me that I must not take any notice of what he said because his mind was wandering, nevertheless it seemed to me that his mind was perfectly clear, and I liked to hear him talk about his travels. He had been in Australia, and this interested me, because I remembered that Uncle Matthew had once said that my mother had gone to Australia.

Suddenly I had an idea. Uncle Matthew had just gone home and Miss Murry was out and Mrs Winter was upstairs. I was quite alone with the old man.

'My mother is in Australia,' I said to him, not too loudly but quite clearly enough for him to hear.

He gave a little jump, as old people do when they are

interrupted in their memories, and muttered to himself for a moment or two.

'Your mother? Mother? The little girl's mother?'

He broke off and fidgeted in his chair; there was a puzzled look in his eyes.

'Yes,' I said boldly. 'My mother went to Australia. Did you ever meet her there?'

He took a hand off the arm of the chair and rubbed at the white bristles on his chin and shook his head slowly as he spoke.

'Australia? I don't think they send them to Australia any more.'

He stopped. I said nothing. I could make nothing of this.

'No, not Australia,' he went on. 'Let me see now, where did they send her? Very sad that it had to come to that. The poor little girl. Poor Ruth. Now let me see. Where was it that they sent her?'

He was gripping the arm of the chair again and staring straight ahead at the opposite wall as if searching there for the answer to his question. But there was nothing there save the picture of the old bridge that Miss Murry liked so much. I could hardly breathe. I felt excited and frightened all at once. It was like the times in the playground at Miss Green-field's school when someone would come up from behind and catch you round the neck and put a hand over your eyes and say in a hoarse voice : 'Guess who.'

'But I'm here now, Mr Murry,' I cried. 'I'm Ruth, and here I am.'

He turned his head slowly and looked at me. 'Poor little Ruth,' he said. 'Poor little baby.'

Suddenly I knew. I had guessed who.

'You mean my mother,' I said as casually as I could. 'My mother's name was Ruth too.'

Nobody had ever told me; I was not supposed to want to know my mother's name.

'Yes, yes,' said the old man impatiently, as if he thought I had been blaming him for not speaking clearly, 'of course your mother's name was Ruth. They called you after her.'

'Am I like her?' I asked.

He did not answer but simply shook his head again and again, saying: 'Poor little girl, poor little girl.'

I waited, hoping he would go on talking aloud to himself. After a while he muttered something that I could not catch and then suddenly, without any warning, he began to bang his stick on the ground. He leaned forward, his eyes opened wider and wider, his mouth moved as if he was chewing something and then it opened wide and he started to shout: 'Let her go – help, help! Let her go!'

I was terrified. I had never seen him like this. He raised his stick and hit out at the air.

'Leave her alone! You'll kill her. Haven't you done harm enough?'

I crept behind his chair. He was swinging the stick wildly about, growing more and more excited. I dared not touch him, I dared not speak. Mrs Winter would hear, and she would blame me for upsetting him, and she would tell Miss Murry and I would never be allowed to speak to the old man again. Just when I really seemed to be finding out something about my mother.

All of a sudden the shouting stopped. He made a funny little noise like water gurgling in the pipes and his head fell forward and his stick dropped to the ground. I ran out of the room to the bottom of the stairs. Mrs Winter appeared at the same moment on the top step.

'What on earth is the matter?' she cried at the same moment as I said: 'Come quick. It's Mr Murry. I think

wanted to be an actress and nothing would stop her. The Scottish cousins had lost touch with her by this time and she had no protector but myself. We quarrelled about it, I'm afraid, and she ran away to London with a schoolfriend and I heard nothing of her for some time. Later I learnt that she had managed to get a small part in a play, but it was largely due to her looks, because she was too stiff and tense to be a good actress. She had lovely red-gold hair and big grey eyes and when she was happy she had enormous vitality and charm, but when she was frustrated and miserable it was a very different story.'

Miss Murry stopped as if expecting me to say something, but I had nothing to say. I simply wanted her to go on. She sighed again.

'It was in London that she met your father. He wrote poems and plays, but I'm afraid he was not much better at that than your mother was at acting. Perhaps this was what brought them together. At any rate it brought me and Ruth together again, for she wrote to me about him and how much she loved him and was sure I would love him too.'

She broke off suddenly and this time there was so long a silence that I was obliged to ask a question to get her started again.

'What happened then?'

'Why, you were born,' she said, and it sounded to me as if she had been crying, 'and about that time the War broke out and your father went into the army and your mother brought you to Rivermead and here you lived. Your father came back for his leaves. Some of them, that is. Sometimes he went to stay somewhere else and that made your poor mother very unhappy.'

'I don't remember my mother being unhappy,' I said. I was growing impatient. I was not at that moment very

D

interested in my father. All I wanted was that Miss Murry should come to the time when I sat learning to read in the big sitting-room, and tell me what happened next and where my mother was now.

'She wasn't unhappy when I was learning to read,' I added.

'Oh – do you remember that?'

She sounded surprised and I glanced up and caught her eye. Just for a moment there was that look in her face, the look that Aunt Bessie had when she told Uncle Matthew that the child had been asking questions again, and in that moment all the little glimmers of knowledge that I had about my mother came together – the secrecy and the fright when I spoke of her, Aunt Bessie's words that I had overheard, Miss Murry's great sadness and now her fear, and above all, Mr Murry's shout : 'Let her alone – you'll kill her!' They all merged into one great flash of under-standing, and somewhere in that flash was the memory of my nightmare, the terrible face in the wall. Something very dreadful had happened to my mother after my reading lessons, something so dreadful that they didn't want me to know. They hoped I had forgotten; they hoped I would never speak of her, and that was why they had kept all memory of her away from me. The bitterness came over me again and for a moment I had the same sort of impulse to punish them all as I had had when I ran from Uncle Matthew's cottage and when I jumped off the wall at St Margaret's School and broke my leg.

But Miss Murry was speaking and what she said made me forgive her.

'What else can you remember?' she asked. 'Would you like to tell me what you remember and then I will fill in the gaps – as far as I know them of course, or would you rather I just tell you in the way I learnt about it myself?'

I caught at her hand which was dangling down to the grass by the side of the deckchair. It felt soft and yet solid and comforting and it closed gently around my own.

'It all comes back at nights,' I said. 'I dream of the red face in the wall.'

It was the first time I had ever told anybody of my dream. As I spoke it seemed to appear before me, in all its horror, right here in the bright riverside garden, with Miss Murry holding my hand. The fear swelled and swelled, as if the very putting it into words had a power over it, and then suddenly it was gone, blown right away with the words I had spoken.

'The red face,' said Miss Murry quietly, not looking at me but holding my hand very tight. 'That is strange, very strange.'

'In the wall,' I cried. 'It suddenly comes out of the wall.'

'The wall?' She sounded puzzled. 'The wall of the boathouse?'

'Yes, yes, the boathouse.'

Of course it was the boathouse. Of course I had always known that I must search for my mother by the river.

'But it's only wooden palings,' said Miss Murry. We both looked down the lawn towards the corner where the little building with its pointed church-like roof stood. 'There's no hole in them, only the door. Ah, wait a moment.'

She too gave the impression of having been struck by a flash of light.

'Of course. The door doesn't go up to the roof. There's a sizeable gap. You can stand outside and look over it. That's it, I expect. When the housekeeper found you she didn't go in but stood and looked over the top of the door. And it had been a very brilliant day. The angle of the evening sun would have just caught her face and reddened it. That's the explanation, I'm sure.'

'Was it Mrs Winter?' I asked. I wanted to ask what it was she had seen, for my memory stopped here, but I was still not quite sure that Miss Murry would tell me the truth unless it seemed that I already knew it.

'No, Ruth. Mrs Winter only came last year. It was Mrs Morrison. She had been with us for a long time, but it was a great shock to her, all the publicity and the trial, and she didn't want to stay on after that.'

'Where did they send my mother?' I asked.

'To a place called Longheath. It's really a sort of hospital, you know, where they send people who have committed crimes when they were so disturbed in their minds that they didn't realize what they were doing.'

'Where is it?' I asked. I didn't look at Miss Murry; my fingers were tugging at the grass and I was hot and cold with excitement. My mother was at Longheath; I could go and see her.

'Where is it, where is it?' I insisted.

'Oh – a long way away. Down in the West Country.'

'But we can go by train. When can we go?'

I stretched out a hand to clutch at hers, but she had shifted in her chair, turning slightly away from me, and was clasping her hands together in her lap. She seemed to have gone off into a dream, as old Mr Murry had done, and to have forgotten me completely.

'When are we going to see my mother?' I asked again.

She turned to face me then but I didn't like the smile on her face. It was too sweet. It was the sort that Aunt Bessie put on for visitors. It was the sort of smile that said to me : 'Here comes a lie.'

'We can't go just yet,' she said, 'because she is not well

enough to be visited. You wouldn't want to go and see
your mother when she was too weak to talk to you, would
you, darling?'

'We could look at her,' I muttered, tugging at the grass
again.

'Better not. Believe me, Ruth, it is really better not. I keep
in touch all the time, you know, and they let me know how
she is, and as soon as she is fit to be visited they will tell me.'

'When will that be? Next week?'

She did not reply and I knew it was hopeless to ask
further, but I had the feeling that she had been going to tell
me more about my mother before I started to ask to go and
visit her, and I thought hard to try to find a question that
would start Miss Murry talking again but that would not
reveal my own ignorance. I remembered Mr Murry's cry
of 'Let her go!' and I remembered Miss Murry saying that
my father had made my mother unhappy.

'What did he do to her?' I asked. 'My father, I mean.
He tried to kill her, didn't he?'

'What makes you say that? Is it something you
remember?'

The sweetness had gone from Miss Murry's voice and
once more there was that note of alarm.

'Didn't he try to kill her?' I persisted.

'I'm afraid,' she said slowly, but whether it was because
she was not telling the truth or because she did not know
the answer I could not tell, 'I'm afraid we shall never know
what really happened at the end. But there had been a lot
of quarrels before that day. Very violent quarrels. They
were both highly strung and under a great strain and the
circumstances were not easy. She was very much in love
with him, and seeing him so seldom, of course all her
feelings were bottled up and then they burst out when

Julian came back on leave. And he had a bad time in the trenches and it did unbalance him, I suppose, although I'm sure he really loved her very much. I expect you can remember hearing them quarrelling. Can you remember that, Ruth?'

I nodded vigorously. It was better to act a lie than say one. In fact I could remember nothing whatever about it.

Miss Murry sighed deeply.

'I was afraid so. It was quite upsetting sometimes. It used to alarm my dear father. I always kept a close watch on you, though, and I whisked you out of the way when it looked as if they were going to have a big row, but on this occasion unfortunately you had already run off to the boathouse by yourself. You weren't supposed to, of course, in case you fell in the water, but you always were a brave explorer for a little girl. You used to shin up trees and climb fences and sit in the dinghy splashing about with a paddle. I rather envied you your freedom,' she added with a smile.

Then she went on : 'On that late autumn day, about two years after the War came to an end, your father came to tell your mother that his regiment was being posted to India. He told me first, hoping, I think, that I would offer to tell her and that he could just creep away without seeing her, but at that moment she came in from the garden, saying you had gone to the kitchen to lick out the bowl from Mrs Morrison's cake-making. Actually you must have gone straight to the boathouse and curled up in the bottom of the punt, for you were not in sight when they came in. Your mother suggested that they should go to the boathouse to talk undisturbed. In their happier times they would take out the punt and laze about in it. That is where they were found – in the punt with the red cushions. Mrs Morrison and I were in the garden when we heard the first shot and we were puzzled as well as alarmed, because your father did not have his army revolver on him, and we did not know then that your mother had a loaded one hidden away. She must have fetched it when she went to get her shawl, and concealed it under her shawl. It was wrong of her, but she always was very nervous. Anyway, when we heard the shot we ran to the boathouse and Mrs Morrison looked over the top of the door. "Go and find the child," I cried. "Keep her away." Of course I didn't know then that you were in the boathouse too.'

She stopped abruptly and put an arm round my shoulders and leaned over so that her head was close to my own.

'Do you remember it, Ruth?' she whispered urgently, her eyes looking keenly into mine.

I wanted to pretend that I did remember, but I dared not. It was so solemn and important that it would have been like trying to lie to God.

'I don't know,' I said, 'but I was very frightened, I know that.'

'Yes, darling.' She hugged me, but it felt as if she was comforting herself as much as comforting me. 'Of course you were frightened. I was very frightened myself. Your father had got the revolver away from your mother and he had fired that first shot – it hit the far wall of the boat-house – and then somehow or other she had got the weapon back. I think he must have tripped when the boat was swaying about and momentarily loosened his grip on it. Just as we rushed in, she fired. He was in the middle of the punt, she was at the far end. The boat was rocking about and making a lot of splashing. I suppose it was that, combined with the shock and the semi-darkness inside after the bright light outside, that accounts for my not noticing at first that you were there. But I was not too late. Thank

God I was not too late.'

She hugged me again and I saw the glisten of tears in her eyes.

And suddenly I could see something else too. It was like a picture in a story – a story out of a book that was more real to me than my life. And yet it seemed that it was indeed my life.

'I fell in the water!' I cried. 'I fell out of the boat into the water and hung on to something – I hung on – I hung on – '

As suddenly as it had come the light failed. What had I hung on to? Had it really happened? Was it only a story after all?

Miss Murry was speaking.

'You hung on to a branch of that big willow-tree that dips into the water at the side of the boathouse. You managed to cling to it for long enough to save yourself, although you had been some time in the water and were unconscious when we found you at last.'

She gave a great sigh.

'Well, my dear, that's how it was. Your father was killed instantly. Your poor mother knelt there with the revolver in her hands and said nothing but, "I killed him, I got it in first." Neither the police nor the doctors could get anything else out of her. She went off into that dream world where she has remained ever since, and that, combined with the uncertainty as to whether he had really tried to kill her first, made them decide in the end that it was best to put her somewhere where she could come to no harm. Of course you had to be asked questions, young as you were, but the shock and the near escape from drowning had affected your memory so much that you had nothing to tell. Mercifully, we all thought. You did ask for your mother at first, but you seemed quite satisfied when we told you she had gone away on a long journey. When it was all over we thought very seriously about your future, and we decided that it would be best for you to grow up in a completely different environment where nobody knew anything about the tragedy. You had always been fond of my gardener, Mr Baines, and he of you. If he adopted you, then at least you would have a familiar face around. We did it for the best, Ruth.'

She moved from her deckchair on to the grass beside me and played with my daisy chains as she went on talking.

'I had watched over you since the day you were born and it was very painful to have to part with you. But everybody here knew all about you and it was too much to hope that they would keep quiet for ever and that you would never hear any rumours. I hoped that it would all be blotted out of your mind and that you could make a fresh start in life, in happier circumstances. But I was wrong and I ought to have known better. I am sorry, Ruth. Will you forgive me and let me try to make it up to you now?'

She dropped the daisy chain and held out her arms and I flung myself against her and we clung together and cried a little, both of us, comforting each other. Of course I was shocked by what she had told me, but I was not very surprised, because in a strange way I felt as if I had always known it.

'It was a very bad time,' she said as she kissed me, 'but it is all over now. You shall stay here with me and be my own little Ruth and nothing shall ever harm you.'

I snuggled up to her because I knew she wanted me to, and indeed it was very wonderful to know that I was to live once more in this lovely house and never be sent away again. Yet the sense of love and safety only lapped me round; it did not warm me through and through. Even as we hugged each other and Miss Murry called me her darling little Ruth over and over again, there was still that hard core of suspicion right inside me that would not be melted. She seemed to have told me the truth about my mother and yet I felt sure that she was holding something back. Why could I not go and see her? Was she really too ill for me to go?

I felt ashamed of these doubts when Miss Murry went in to fetch some photographs of my parents for me to look at.

'But where is the wedding photograph?' I asked.

I knew there ought to be a wedding photograph, because Uncle Matthew and Aunt Bessie had one which stood on the piano. I never liked it; I thought they both looked stiff and silly. But I would have liked to see how my mother and father looked in their wedding photograph.

'It was taken away,' said Miss Murry, 'when your mother's possessions were packed up.'

She spoke too quickly. I felt sure she was lying but I pretended to believe, partly because I truly loved her and partly because it seemed safest to. It was so wonderful, this home of mine, that I tried hard to stifle the deep restless questioning inside me. But it would not be stilled, and every now and then the dream came back and left me with a great empty horror that none of the joys of the sweet riverside home with my kind guardian could fill.

CHAPTER VII

I DID not go to Miss Murry's school after all, but to another school where the headmistress was a friend of hers. She put the alternatives to me as from one grown-up to another.

'If you come to St Margaret's,' she said, 'I shall have to treat you particularly severely so that the other girls don't suspect me of favouring you. But even then it will place you apart from the others. They won't feel free to say rude things about me if you are there. But if you go to Freelands as a weekly boarder you will be just like all the other girls there and I can bring you home every weekend. It's up to you to choose, though. As regards teaching, I think both schools are of about the same standard.'

I chose Freelands because I liked the name and because I knew that was what she wanted me to do.

'If you don't mind, my dear,' she said some time later, 'I am going to suggest you take my name. It will make it much simpler for us both from so many points of view. Would you mind very much being called Ruth Murry?'

I did mind, terribly. It seemed a betrayal of my own father and mother, even if they never knew of it. And it seemed to be taking some of my very own self away from me – the self that had proudly and carefully written 'Ruth Baines' in the few books I could call my own. But of course 'Ruth Baines' was not my name. I had continued to think of myself as that even after Miss Murry told me about my parents, and the shock of realization that came to me now was as bad as the shock of the earlier occasion. Who was I, that I did not even have a name? I could not speak. Miss

Murry did not seem to notice that I was upset.

'What's in a name, as Shakespeare says,' she went on. 'It's only a convenience, after all. And you'll still have your Christian name, the one they chose for you.'

'Did they choose it?' I asked suddenly, and the hurt inside me rejoiced at Miss Murry's look of distress. 'Perhaps they didn't even trouble to choose me a name. Perhaps somebody just called me my mother's name for convenience.'

She caught me up and hugged me.

'My darling child. My dear little Ruth. You must not say such things.'

Then she put me down and said: 'It is very dreadful to hear such bitterness in a child not yet ten years old. But you have good cause for resentment. Fate has given you a wretched start in life. I only wish I knew what on earth I could do to try to counteract it.'

She looked and sounded so unhappy that of course I leapt at her, of my own accord this time, and kissed her and thanked her again and again and said that I loved her name, always had loved it ever since Uncle Matthew told me about her school garden.

'But you must stop calling me Miss Murry,' she said presently. 'My name is Annette, but I only use it when I want to be very formal. Perhaps you had better call me Nan, as my father does. Would that do?'

'Yes,' I said, and then feeling I ought to say something more, I added: 'Yes, Nanny.'

That was the way it came out and she did not object. So when I went to Freelands School I answered the roll-call as Ruth Murry and when I talked about my home to the other girls I always referred to 'Nanny', and some of them seemed to think she was my grandmother and some of them thought she was an aunt and some thought she was my nursemaid. If anybody asked outright who she was I replied : 'Oh, she's just Nanny.'

In fact I rather enjoyed making a mystery. It gave me a feeling of importance and power and made up for the fact that I didn't live in London and have a father who worked at something high up in the Navy or a mother whose photograph was in the society papers and who had been to tea with the King and Queen. But it also meant that I had no friends, none who were even as near to me as silly little Minnie at the village school at Littleford had been. At first I thought that because the girls had beautiful clothes and seemed to know all about what went on in the world, that they must be very clever; but when I found that they had not read the books that I had read and could not work out the problems that I could, I began to despise them instead of admiring and fearing them. So I became brainy Ruth, whom it was better not to sneer at and torment, in case she refused to do your algebra for you or deliberately did it wrong.

And so the years went by. I was lonely but did not feel it. In the long summer holidays I would spend hours lying on the lawn or in the punt at Rivermead, dreaming or reading. Sometimes I sat by the bedside of old Mr Murry, who lingered on pitifully for years, and listened to his wandering talk, the scrapbook of his life. I never again risked asking him outright about my parents, but every now and then he came out with little snippets of his own accord and I put them away in my mental storehouse.

About three years after I entered Freelands School, Miss Murry told me that my mother was dead. I had long since given up asking whether I could go and see my mother. It was always the same reply : Wait a little, then she will be better and you will be older. Once or twice I thought of making my own way to Longheath, but I had grown old enough to understand that even a child of twelve could not hope to undertake such a journey on her own. Besides, I had no longer the courage to attempt it, for with growing knowledge came growing apprehension; I was nervous and saw difficulties where as a child of eight I had seen none. Much though I despised my schoolfellows and held myself aloof from them, nevertheless I had taken on some of their attitudes, and when Miss Murry said, as we were driving home one Friday evening, that she had heard from the prison hospital, my first reaction was a little stab of horrified revulsion at the word 'prison' and only after that did I think of my mother.

'It's bad news, I'm afraid, Ruth darling,' she said.

She spoke in the too sweet voice that I always suspected and that always brought out the very worst in me.

'Who has she shot this time?' I asked viciously, determined to shock and hurt her.

I felt her tense up and the car swerved slightly. She righted it and replied: 'Please don't talk like that, Ruth. You know I dislike it. Your mother has done no harm to anyone at Longheath. She has been confused in her mind but perfectly quiet all the time she has been there, but her health has rapidly failed and she died last week of a severe lung infection.'

We had come out of a side road on to the broad new road and Miss Murry suddenly made the car go so fast that it took my breath away.

'Oh,' I said, 'she's dead.'

I didn't really take it in at all. I felt only excitement at being rushed along so quickly. We had never before gone at such a speed.

'Oh,' I said again after a minute or two. 'Will she be buried?'

'Of course,' snapped Miss Murry.

'Where?'

'On the spot, of course,' she replied in the same angry tones. Then she let the car slow down, rather to my disappointment, and said in a new sort of voice, neither the over-sweet one that I disliked, nor the kind strong one that I relied on, nor the sad one that made me feel guilty, but a worried anxious voice that I was to hear more and more of as the years went on: 'Ruth, my dear, I am very sorry to sound so unsympathetic, but you are really very difficult to talk to sometimes. Of course you can't be expected to mourn your mother's death and in fact there is really no reason why you should even be told about it, but I thought it right that you should know.'

'Do I go to the funeral?' I asked.

I didn't really ask this in order to plague her further, but I was beginning to feel rather queer and didn't know what to say.

'Of course not,' she snapped again. 'There can be no question of it.'

And then, after a minute or two, as if repenting, she added in the new voice: 'These things are done very quietly, you see. It is very distressing even for an adult and they certainly would not let a child be present. I know it is very upsetting for you, but really there is nothing to be done about it. Nothing whatever. I really cannot see what else I could have done.'

She was talking more to herself than to me but I could feel how anxiously she was waiting for my response. I ought to have burst into tears so that she could have stopped the car to kiss me and tell me that I was to look on her as a mother. But I could not cry although I longed to do so, and I could not allow her to comfort me although I badly needed comfort, for there was too much falseness between us. I had no fears that she might desert me. Even if I became much more unruly than I already was, she would do her duty by me. But duty it was. She loved me from the head and not the heart. Young as I was I could tell that, but I could not let her see I knew because I dared not spoil the only love I had. So I kept silent for the rest of the way, since I could neither be myself nor play the role she wished me to.

When we got back I was going to run straight up to my room but she put an arm round my shoulders and said: 'Just a minute, darling, there's something I want to give you.'

It was her honest voice again and my mind instantly jumped to the notion that she had some little possession of my mother's, perhaps a piece of jewellery that she had been allowed to keep in prison or that had been put away safely for her. The thought made my heart leap with excitement and when the gift turned out to be the few snapshots that I had already seen, I blamed Miss Murry bitterly in my mind for my self-created disappointment, and the tears came at last but I would not let her follow me to my room.

I pushed the photographs to the back of a drawer without even looking at them and then I sat on my bed and clenched my hands together and scolded myself for breaking the rule of never expecting anything so that I would never be disappointed. I tensed myself into toughness and found a grim satisfaction in appearing to be unfeeling. Only when Uncle Matthew spoke to me did the defences crack. He had become rather shy of me since I had grown up into a young lady, as he called it, but he showed that he had been told the news about my mother by remarking the following morning, when I went to help him in the garden : 'Those scarlet poppies were your mother's favourite. She liked things big and bright and glowing.'

I flung my arms round him and shivered uncontrollably, although it was a warm morning, and he patted my shoulders and said, 'Easy now, easy now,' again and again.

After that I felt more able to behave as Miss Murry wanted me to, and indeed there were many hours when I hardly thought about my parents at all, for my life was becoming very full of activity, both at school and at home.

CHAPTER VIII

THE HEADMISTRESS of Freelands School decided that I was to be turned into a scholar and so I was given a lot of extra work to do at weekends. In the holidays Miss Murry took me to plays and concerts and art exhibitions, and for short visits to London and to Paris. Then there were the visitors to the house – teachers, artists, writers, people in public life, people who had travelled abroad – there seemed to be no end of them and they talked endlessly. She always introduced me as 'my dear adopted daughter Ruth', and I never let her down on these occasions, but would stand there simpering suitably. Some of the visitors just smiled in a vague way and were obviously anxious to get back to their conversation, but others took the trouble to talk to me and to answer my questions.

Among this latter group was the man who had found me on the towing-path about to fall into the river and had brought me to Miss Murry's school. Professor Nicholas West. Soon I came to realize that he was not as old as his big horn-rimmed glasses and his title of 'Professor' had at first made him seem. I learnt that he taught English literature to university students, and from the way the other visitors treated him I got the idea that he was cleverer than they were and that they were a little envious of him but too polite to say so. And again, like myself, he didn't seem quite to belong. Most of the others talked in a rather superior, drawling way, as if they knew everything but found it a great effort to say it, but Professor West spoke quickly: the words poured out in a rush when he got excited and it sometimes seemed that he might be in danger of dropping his aitches, although I never actually heard this happen. What he did forget, though, were his drawing-room table manners. There were about four or five of them sitting one day in Miss Murry's big room and Mrs Winter had asked me to take in the tea-trolley, because she was very busy with the old man upstairs. As I pushed the trolley through the door they all called out: 'Ah! Here comes the tea-lady.'

There was a little laugh and Miss Murry gave me an encouraging smile and then they all went on talking; but Professor West got up and took my hand and pushed me down on a stool by the chair where he was sitting. I felt rather shy and out of it, so I just sat there and watched him drink his tea. There were some hard crisp biscuits, and all the others were crumbling them in their fingers and taking little mouthfuls and looking rather uncomfortable about it, but Professor West just picked his up and dipped it in his teacup, as Uncle Matthew used to do, and then bit off the soft, tea-soaked half of the biscuit.

Another time, when I was about thirteen years old, I had

managed to get the punt out of the boathouse and had tied it up to a tree-root at the bottom of the lawn. I was standing in it, poking at the bottom of the river with the pole and wishing somebody would show me how to use it properly, when I heard a loud shout.

'Oi! Wait for me.'

It was Professor West.

'Can't stand it another minute,' he said as he came to the water's edge and jumped into the punt. 'These high-class intellectual socialists and all their blueprints for Utopia.'

He untied the rope, grabbed the pole from my hands, prodded at the root and gave a great push so that we sped off down the river.

'Talking about the rights and dignity of the working man when they've never done a hand's turn in their lives. Not they. Not bloody likely.'

He was pink in the face and very excited. The punt pole hit the gravel bottom of the river with a loud crunchy plop and we shot forward again.

After a little while I said : 'But aren't you a socialist too? I thought we all were, all of us here, I mean. Not at my school, of course. They're a frightful lot there.'

He looked down at me as if he had realized for the first time that he had an audience and was not just speaking his mind to himself.

'Of course I am. But *I* have good reason to be.'

'Why?' I asked.

He gave a groan. 'The classic case of the underprivileged self-made boy. Left school at thirteen – father a farm labourer. University extension classes and Ruskin College. Trade union courses and scholarships. The War and an unexpected chance for patriotic promotion. The whole bloody boring works in fact. I've made it. Here I am within the sacred portals, unlike poor old Jude. Hardy Professor of Eng. Lit. in the University of Oxford – the one and only chance in the academic world for a working-class boy, and that's no thanks to my fellow-countrymen but simply due to the generosity of a self-made American millionaire. They want his money so they put up with his conditions. The formalities are complied with. The working boy turned academic is even regarded with mild interest. A curious zoological specimen – will it bite? What does it eat? But it is always made perfectly clear – oh so very discreetly – that this old-school-tieless intruder can never be a true member of the club. Even among that gang of lily-fingered revolutionaries back there.'

He waved an arm wildly in the direction of Miss Murry's house, stumbled, and nearly followed the punt pole into the water. I couldn't help laughing at his language and at his antics, although I tried not to because I didn't want to hurt him.

'Go on!' he cried. 'Laugh away. I'm a funny ass, aren't I?'

I tried to deny it but he shouted me down.

'I don't suppose you've the least idea what I'm talking about.'

'I have!' I cried indignantly. 'I know just what you mean. I'm an outsider too. I'll never be a member of the club either.'

'Nonsense,' he retorted, 'you're bang in the middle of the salon. Heiress and beloved protégée of the grande dame herself.'

His French pronunciation was atrocious. Even I, from my little eminence of a twice-weekly session with the school mademoiselle, could tell that. But it didn't matter. I had

from him, as from none of the other learned men and
women whom I met, the impression of an extraordinary
power-house of a brain whose wheels simply would not keep
turning steadily as they ought but kept stopping and starting and going backwards and sideways and sending off
sparks in all directions, so that you felt as if any moment
now it would all go up in a glorious blaze.

I very nearly told him then what I really felt about Miss
Murry and about my plan to find out everything about
my parents when I was grown up, but I stopped myself just
in time. He is angry with them now because they have dis-
agreed with him, I said to myself, but he will get over it
and they will be friends again and then he will tell Miss
Murry all I have said. I was glad afterwards that I told him
nothing because it was just about that time that I realized
Miss Murry was in fact very fond of him although she
scolded him a lot and called him a 'daft lad' in a voice that
was meant to be funny but that rather made me squirm.

He never spoke about her friends quite so critically
again, although we went on the river several times alone
together and he taught me to punt and to paddle properly.
I learnt a lot about his childhood and about how the world
had got to be changed if the War was not to have been
fought in vain, and I also learnt that everything was wrong
with the educational system and that I had got to do something about it when I was grown up. Girls in particular
were still not being given enough scope or enough challenge;
even those in charge of an enlightened woman like Miss
Murry were still being brought up to look pretty and to
cook nice meals when the cook was on holiday and to listen
quietly when important subjects like politics and money
were being discussed and never to have any opinions of their
own.

I instantly disproved this assertion of his by saying firmly :
'I'm not being brought up like that.'

'Just like a woman,' he retorted. 'Takes everything
personally. You're as bad as all the rest.'

'And my mother wasn't brought up like that either,' I
said.

It was very exciting to be treated by him as an equal, as
if I were grown up too, but it was also very overwhelming
and I was hard put to it to stand up for myself. He sobered
down instantly, however, at the mention of my mother, so
that I guessed he had been told the story.

'Well, yes,' he said, 'but that's not a very good example
of what I mean.'

'Did you ever meet my mother?' I asked eagerly.

'No, child. I've only known your honoured guardian for
a few years. Since the day you yourself introduced us, in
fact.'

'Oh.' Somehow I had got the idea from Miss Murry
that she and Professor West were very old friends. I
pondered over this and it made me uneasy. It linked up
with things she sometimes said about people that I later
discovered were not exactly untrue but would have given
you a very wrong impression of those people if you had not
met them yourself or if you had not heard what somebody
else thought of them. Professor West, on the other hand,
always said exactly where he had been or what he had done
or what he thought of people, and I often wished he had
been the one who knew the whole truth about my parents.
I could have talked to him as I had never been able to talk
to Miss Murry.

It was this ever-increasing feeling of mistrust that led me
to behave to her in what she called a 'difficult' way. I heard
less and less of her straight firm voice and more and more

of the sweet voice and the self-defensive one. She never spoke unkindly to me but the older I grew and the taller I grew, the more did she call me her 'darling little Ruth', and she treated me at the age of fifteen as less of an equal than she had done when I first came to live with her. When Professor West was there she always managed to make me appear particularly awkward and childish. If he didn't know me, I thought, he really would think me a very silly and immature girl. Sometimes I wished that he would stand up for me against Miss Murry, but he seemed very anxious not to offend her, and I had to be content with little snatches of true companionship with him on the occasions when Miss Murry was otherwise occupied.

He helped me with my studies and gave me many books, among which was a volume of poems by men whose lives had been cut short by the War. Somehow or other I conceived the notion that one of these tragic young poets had been my own father. The idea had a great appeal for me and it was not, after all, quite out of the question, since Miss Murry had once told me that my father had written poetry. I longed to tell Professor West about this but dared not do so for fear he might mention it to Miss Murry. When I returned to school after the long holidays, however, I asked the English mistress for a book that would tell me about the War poets' lives. We got on well enough together in a superficial way, within that tiny upper layer of thought and feeling to which most of my relationships with other people were confined; she found a book for me and I read it eagerly. One of the poets had died tragically and mysteriously of a shooting accident shortly after the end of the War. No details were given; there was no mention of a wife or child, and there was no photograph. Only one of his poems was included in my collection – a love poem, tragic and mysterious too. I got it by heart and found it very beautiful although I did not fully understand it.

But after that I did not know how to proceed. The English mistress could help me no more, and I thought it would look suspicious if I kept on pestering her. The only person whom it seemed safe to ask was Uncle Matthew. Aunt Bessie had died and he lived all by himself in the cottage. I had a bicycle now and was free to come and go as I liked, so I cycled over to see him. I said nothing about the poem but just asked casually while we were washing up the tea-things: 'Uncle Matthew, did you ever meet my father?'

He was startled into admitting that he had.

'What was he like?'

'Very fine – very fine-looking indeed in his officer's uniform.'

'I know that,' I cried impatiently. 'I've got his photograph.'

But was it really his photograph? My suspicion of Miss Murry was such that for a moment I wondered whether she had simply pacified me by giving me the photographs of two complete strangers.

'What did he look like?' I went on quickly. 'Dark? Long straight nose, keen-looking eyes?'

Uncle Matthew shook his little grey head and frowned. 'Could be, could be,' he muttered.

'And what was his name?'

Miss Murry had referred to him as 'Julian', but for all I knew that too was a lie. The poet in the anthology had written under a pseudonym – a Greek name – so that was no help.

Uncle Matthew looked at me pathetically with his fading eyes. 'His name? Now let me see. He's getting very old and forgetful, your poor old uncle. You must be patient with him, little Ruth.'

'Little Ruth' was now considerably taller than Mr Matthew Baines, but it was impossible to be angry with him. He was not, like Miss Murry, trying to show me up in a false light; he simply thought of me as a little girl still. But no amount of gentle prodding could extract a name from him and I was inclined to think that he had genuinely forgotten. I did, however, learn two things : Uncle Matthew had not been at Rivermead on the day of the accident, and Mrs Morrison, who had been housekeeper then, had gone to live with her married daughter in Australia.

That's where Australia comes in, I thought grimly; they had to concoct a story to tell me so they used scraps of things that had really happened because they hadn't the imagination to invent it all.

'It is true, isn't it,' I said, 'that my mother did shoot my father and that she was shut away in a prison for the criminally insane?'

'Oh dear, oh dear. Yes, I believe so,' he said unhappily. 'How strange it is to hear you talk like this.'

'Well, it's some comfort to have your confirmation of that,' I exclaimed. 'Now, Uncle. I want to go to the prison where my mother died. There must be people there who will remember her and will be able to tell me something about her. They can't refuse to talk to me. I'm her nearest relative. Will you help me, please? I don't know how to set about it on my own.'

Of course he replied that it was not for him, but for Miss Murry, whose ward I was, to decide on such an important matter, and he became so distressed when I persisted that in the end I had to allow the subject to drop.

I turned then to the idea of Mrs Winter, the housekeeper,

as a possible ally. She was a motherly soul, much given to baking cakes for me and trying to fatten me up. She knew something of my history and she had attended to old Mr Murry and heard him talk before the arrival of the nurse who was now a permanent fixture in the house. I had more or less made up my mind to put on a pathetic act and appeal to Mrs Winter, when two events took place that brought my deteriorating relationship with Miss Murry to the pitch of crisis.

The first was the departure of Professor West to America for a year's visit. This was a great blow to both Miss Murry and myself, but we pretended to each other that we were delighted that he should have this opportunity, which he very much wanted, of lecturing on the other side of the Atlantic. Then came the second shock to our already secretly mourning household: the old man died at last. He had been dying by inches during all those bedridden years, and for the last months he had lain speechless and almost motionless, a poor stricken tree that was not allowed to crumble away at nature's call, but was watered and drained at regular intervals as if it were a young sapling with the promise of green and vigorous life ahead.

It made little difference to the household, apart from the departure of the nurse and the conversion of his bedroom into another guest-room, and yet the whole place felt changed, and not for the better, after he had gone.

Miss Murry became very silent and moody, and I could only suppose that she was mourning deeply, although in fact she had often said how much she longed for her father to be released. But one day she said to a cousin who had come to help turn out the old man's things: 'All those wasted years – no life for him, and no hope for me.'

The cousin, a pleasant-looking elderly lady, looked

surprised, and said : 'I know it's been a great tie for you, Nan, but surely not all that bad. You've had excellent help, and it's never affected your career.'

'My career!' cried Miss Murry bitterly, with a look on her face such as I had never seen there before. 'That's all you all think of. It never seems to occur to anybody to wonder how many chances of a happy marriage I might have had to forgo.'

'But, my dear.'

The cousin glanced at me before speaking further. They were standing by the tall bureau in the sitting-room, where Mr Murry's books and papers had lain untouched during all his helpless years, and I was curled up on the window-seat, reading as usual.

'I wonder if Ruth would mind making some tea, as Mrs Winter is out,' went on the cousin. 'I could do with a little break.'

It was an obvious excuse to get rid of me, but Miss Murry did not take it up; in fact she seemed oblivious of my presence.

'Yes, marriage,' she went on in a harsh voice. 'I couldn't pack up and go to America, with Dad like that, could I? And now I've gone and saddled myself with yet another burden.'

'Hush, dear,' said the cousin, again glancing at me.

But it was too late. All the unspoken resentment that had been simmering in me for so long suddenly swelled up and burst through the tight bonds of gratitude that had been holding it down. I flung away my book, jumped up from the window-seat, and cried : 'I'm sorry I'm such a burden and nuisance to everyone. It's not really my fault, since I didn't ask to be born. But it's a great pity, since nobody seems to want me, that when my mother killed my father she didn't kill me too.'

I could say no more. My voice was shaking too much. I stood there, in the beautiful room with the windows overlooking the river, with my hands twisting together in front of me, struck still with horror at what I had said, and seeing that horror reflected on the two faces turned in my direction.

'Now that's a very wicked thing to say, Ruth,' said Miss Murry at last. 'You must never talk like that. You mustn't even think like that. Of course I don't think of you as a burden. I was thinking of something else, not of you at all, when I said that just now.'

I didn't believe her. She had certainly been thinking of me and her cousin's anxious looks had given her away.

Miss Murry stepped towards me and held out her arms : 'My darling little Ruth,' she began.

'I'm not your darling and I'm not little !' I cried violently, jumping behind an armchair so that she could not get at me. 'And I haven't even any proof that Ruth is my name. Where is my birth certificate? Why have I never seen it? Was I born in prison? Was I born in a lunatic asylum? Who am I? What am I? You say my mother went mad. How do you know I'm not mad myself?'

The voice rose to a scream and went on and on, quite out of my control, but at the same time something in me shuddered to know that the voice was my own.

'Perhaps I am really mad. Is that what you're afraid of? That I'll kill someone, turn into a murderess like my mother. Is that why you sent me away? Is that why Aunt Bessie was so afraid of me, and the teachers at school too, and even Uncle Matthew, and you, you, *you* !'

The voice reached its climax of fury.

'You're all afraid of me. I see it all now.'

Suddenly the hysteria stopped and I began to laugh, quite calmly.

'That's it, of course. You're afraid how I may turn out, afraid what I may find out. That's why I have to be little Ruth. That's why I must never grow up.'

I came round to the front of the chair, confident now that Miss Murry would not try to embrace me.

'Well, you needn't worry any longer. I'll take myself and my evil inheritance and my dangerous curiosity right out of your way. I'll get a teaching job. I'll be a nursemaid. I'll earn my keep scrubbing floors if that's the only way. And you can go off to America and find Professor West and marry him if that's what you want.'

I heard her give a gasp and as I looked back from the doorway, to which I had been moving as I spoke, I saw that she had sunk into a chair and that her cousin was leaning over her. I had a little prick of conscience then, but the great flood of bitterness and fury sped me on. I could not hit out at my fate; I could only hit at Miss Murry, who had done me much good, and as far as I knew, very little wrong. But I had to blame someone and she was the nearest. I didn't want love; I didn't want sympathy, kindness and understanding; I wanted only revenge.

I rushed up to my room and locked the door and lay on the bed sobbing and trembling. The question that I had flung at Miss Murry in order to hurt her continued to echo in my mind. Was I really not quite sane? Had I inherited madness, or developed it as a result of the terrible events that had robbed me of my former self? If only there were somebody whom I could ask, someone whom I could really trust. If only Professor West were not away.

But perhaps I could write to him. I got up from my bed,

found pen and paper, seated myself at the table, and tried
to imagine what he was doing at this moment. I could see
his face clearly against a confused background of sky-
scrapers and loud check suits and big cigars.

'Am I going mad?' I said aloud. 'Am I? Am I?'

And just as my mind had created his image, so it
conjured up his voice with the reply.

'Of course not, Ruth. You're as sane as they make them.
Snap out of it, girl. Use your reason. It's a very good one.'

I smiled faintly to myself. Of course that was what he
would say. Use your reason. Don't ask if you are mad, ask
something more useful.

Why did Miss Murry want me to remain 'little Ruth',
for instance; was she jealous of me as a possible rival, or
was she afraid I might find out that she had not told me
the truth? Why was I so sure that she was concealing
something? Had I any evidence for this suspicion? The
questions flowed along and the very effort of framing them
brought me into a calmer state of mind. Grimacing with
concentration, I forced myself to go back over my life – the
years at school and at Rivermead, the months at Littleford,
and the misty time before that. How much could I really
remember of those earliest years and how many of my
impressions were the result of Miss Murry's prompting?

I lingered longest of all over this last and most difficult
question, searching for the flaw in her story, the place where
her version of my experiences did not fully agree with my
own. It was all to no avail. There was too little to go on.
If I ruthlessly discarded everything that I might conceivably
have imagined or have been told, I was left with only three
certainties: I had learnt to read in Miss Murry's sitting-
room; I had fallen in the water and clung to the willow-
branch; and something had happened to leave indelibly

imprinted on my mind the image of the face in the nightmare.

Two of these items fitted well enough into Miss Murry's story, but the third did not. She had suggested an explanation, but it did not seem to me to be adequate. She had left something out, and this something was the crux of the whole mystery of my being.

CHAPTER IX

OF COURSE I apologized to Miss Murry and we patched it up somehow between us, because I knew that my notion of earning my living was only a fantasy. No one at school would help me; they would not dream of offending Miss Murry. Besides, I should never be able to explain. They only took nice girls at Freelands School, girls whose fathers were quoted in *The Times* and whose mothers were photographed for the *Tatler*. They didn't take murderer's daughters. If I were to try to tell my story it would be as embarrassing for me and my listeners as if I were to strip off all my clothes and dance about stark naked in the middle of school assembly. Such indecent revelations were quite out of the question.

Thus I reasoned to myself in my bitterness and ignorance, and as we grew to young ladyhood and my schoolmates talked more and more of clothes and 'coming out' and husbands and houses in town, the gap between them and myself grew wider and wider. The nearer they came to putting all book-learning behind them for ever, the less important was I as a solver of problems in algebra. I tried to keep my end up by mocking their hopes and joys.

'All done up like a dog's dinner,' I exclaimed spitefully when one of the more sentimental girls was languishing over a magazine article and dreaming aloud of her own wedding-day. I sat down beside her at the table in the big schoolroom where we older girls were allowed to amuse ourselves on winter evenings, put my finger on the illustration at which she was looking, and began to imitate her voice.

'Oh isn't that just too sweet!' I drawled. 'A little page-boy all in white satin. I shall have a little satin page-boy too. But I won't have the roses for my bouquet because I always think orange blossom is the nicest, isn't it? It's so much more like a wedding, isn't it? And I'll have a longer veil because that looks better on a bride, doesn't it, and perhaps just one spray of flowers in my hair.'

I broke off, suddenly aware that the usual birdlike chatter that went on in the room had ceased and that there was no other sound save that of my own viciously mimicking voice and a loud sobbing sniff from Cynthia, my victim. She pulled the magazine away, got up from the table and took herself off to the far end of the room, where she sat hunched up with her hands over her ears, staring at the magazine on her lap, and giving more loud sniffs.

She was a stupid, lethargic girl, with a dull, podgy, pale face, nobody's favourite, and all hopes of her achieving her ambitions must have rested not on her own merits but on the wealth and influence of her financier father. I was a good actress – was I not always acting? – and I had played the part only too well.

There was a hostile silence. I pulled my book towards me and tried to read, but the words made no sense. Should I leave the room? Should I apologize? In my heart I wanted to comfort Cynthia who, like myself, was suffering and alone, but I dared not go to her while none of the others moved.

The silence continued and I could feel my heart thumping. Every bit of me was tight with apprehension. And then, as if some invisible signal had passed between them, they all broke out together like a flock of birds, excited and shrill.

'I'm going to have orange blossom too!'

'And so am I!'

'And a page-boy –'

'And a long veil –'

'A real wedding –'

'With Mendelssohn and all –'

'And a three-tier cake –'

'And six bridesmaids –'

'Mine will be all in pink –'

Like the preceding silence, it seemed to go on for a long time. I wanted to put my hands over my ears but dared not : this was something that I was intended to hear. Eventually it died away as suddenly as it had begun, but one voice carried on beyond the others, high and clear.

'If somebody had had a proper wedding at the proper time then somebody else wouldn't have been a bastard and wouldn't be quite so sarky about weddings now.'

They all looked at me, including the girl who had spoken – Gillian, daughter of a newspaper proprietor, the only one in the class besides myself who had any pretensions to scholarship. We ought to have been friends, and in fact we were sometimes able to talk to each other, but I was usually a little ahead of her in lessons, and when I had written a good essay and hers was not quite so good, she would swing violently round to the side of the philistines. Her last English essay had been marked considerably lower than my own.

There was a little gasp from the other girls: this time it was Gillian who was going too far. The tone of her voice told me that she was getting at me, although I did not at first take in the full meaning of her words. I felt mainly relief at having someone of my own strength to attack, instead of the wretched Cynthia.

'And just what do you mean by that?' I asked very coolly, closing my book and staring at her.

She stared coldly back. 'Our mysterious Nanny,' she said, 'alias Miss Annette Murry, highly revered head of St Margaret's School. That's what I mean by that.'

'Well, what about her?'

My hands gripped the book. It was a thin volume of poetry and it began to bend within my clasp. Gillian looked around the group, seeking their approval, before she replied. But they didn't egg her on; they were tense and frightened. The sympathy of the mob was veering round yet again, and this time it seemed to be coming to rest on me. It was hateful. I didn't want pity; I wanted the truth.

'What about Miss Murry?' I repeated savagely. I dropped the book and began to edge round the table to where Gillian was standing. Two girls moved aside, looking at me in apprehension, and as I approached Gillian she backed away.

'Oh, it's nothing really,' she said feebly. 'It's probably not true. I'm sorry, Ruth. I didn't mean to say anything.'

She retreated as she spoke, merging into the little group of girls who had risen from their chairs and were standing huddled together at the end of the table. It was I who now stood alone.

'You coward!' I yelled. 'You called me a bastard. Of course you meant it. I'll make you talk!'

Gillian began to scream. 'Hold her, hold her! Don't let

her get at me! She's mad. She'll murder me. Mad like her father!'

I shook off the hands that were trying to hold me back and I stood dead still, staring at Gillian's trembling figure.

'Like my father?' I repeated, momentarily fixed in surprise that she had named the wrong parent. 'I'll want you to explain that too.'

Perhaps I really would have attacked her with hand and tooth and nail. I was less hysterical than when I had accused Miss Murry, but much more coldly desperate. Fortunately the teacher on duty that evening heard the shouting and came to investigate. It was the English mistress, the somewhat formidable middle-aged lady who was kindly disposed towards me.

'Oh, it's you lot,' she said, looking at us disdainfully. 'I thought from the noise that you must have handed the room over to the junior school.' Her mouth twitched as it always did when she was trying not to smile. 'Are you playing charades?' she went on. 'Or is this an unscheduled rehearsal? You all look most frightfully dramatic, but I can't place the scene in any play that we have been doing recently.'

The group of girls broke up in shamefaced mutterings and the English mistress stepped back to the door.

'Oh, by the way, Ruth,' she said as if in afterthought, 'I've found that article I promised you. It's in last week's *Times Lit. Sup.* If you'll come along to my room now you can have it straight away.'

I could hear a sigh of relief go up as I left the room, and I too was exceedingly grateful that worse scandal had been averted. I took the newspaper, dreading to be asked further questions and to be drawn into an embarrassing personal relationship with this woman whose scholarship I admired and whose calm goodwill was a great source of comfort to me. But she only asked me to return the paper in a couple of days and then wished me good night. It was her matter-of-fact attitude at that moment that enabled me to endure the rest of the term.

I apologized to Cynthia and made a special effort to win her goodwill. She was grateful for attention from anybody and she soon began to drift around after me as previously she had hung round the biggest social successes in the class. Gillian and the other girls treated me with cold politeness and the subject of my origins was never referred to again in my presence. But they didn't trouble to curb their tongues for Cynthia's sake, in fact they often did not even notice that she was there, and thus it was that I learnt through Cynthia what the others were saying about me in my absence.

As far as I could make out, the story had been brought to Freelands School by one of the maids who had a friend who worked at St Margaret's School. Speculation as to the true identity of the headmistress's protégée had, it seemed, gone on at St Margaret's for years. It had never occurred to me, in my naïve self-centredness, that Miss Murry too might have suffered from inquisitive tongues, and I felt a little qualm of guilt about my own unkindness to her, which speedily turned into fresh resentment at always having to be so grateful. The theory that I was her own natural daughter had apparently been mooted from the very first, and in spite of firm rebuttals by older members of staff who remembered my mother, it popped up again and again to be re-told to every batch of new arrivals – teachers, pupils, and domestic staff alike. Presumably it had been carried not only to Freelands but to other schools and colleges and households as well.

As I prised the precious shreds of information out of the stolid Cynthia, pretending of course that I knew it all already and only wanted to check how much the other girls knew, I found myself wondering again and again whether Professor West had ever heard the rumour. The wildest thoughts shot through my head. He and Miss Murry. Had he lied when he said that he had met her for the first time through me, lied for her own sake? How old was she? About fifty now, I guessed. Thirty-four when I was born. Young enough. And how old was he? Probably not much more than thirty-four now. Take away my sixteen years; old enough at eighteen, but surely not very likely.

At this point my feelings revolted, refusing to admit the possibility of this hateful notion being true, and my reason backed them up. It was just conceivable that Miss Murry had had a child, that its birth had been hushed up under cover of leave of absence owing to illness, and that one of her pupils who owed her a debt of gratitude and had no near relatives to concern themselves about her, had agreed to accept the child as her own. But it was not conceivable that my funny temperamental professor could be the child's father. If he had been, then I should have been told quite a different story, something much simpler than all that rigmarole about the shooting in the boathouse. Why make all that up if it had no basis in fact? Besides, I myself remembered the boathouse and the willow-branch. Something had happened to me there; that much I knew was true. And the photographs of my parents – the beautiful girl and the dark, clever young man. They had to be mine, whatever sins they had committed, whatever their crimes.

The story of the shooting and of my mother's madness that had filled me with horror when first I heard it, and that had kept me apart, in dark and guilty mystery and ignorance, throughout my school years, now appeared to me as my most cherished possession. It was terrible but it was my own. Suppose the shooting of the man and the girl's subsequent insanity were facts, that I had indeed been present at the fatal moment, but that I had not been their child? This thought struck me with fresh horror, but I looked at it closely and found it to be impossible. I remembered the day when Miss Murry had told me. I could see the lawn stretching down to the river and I could feel the daisy-chain in my hands. It had hurt her to tell me; she had acted from a sense of duty and had intended me nothing but good. She was not cruel. Only a thoroughly cruel woman could have told such a story to a child in order to cover up her own secret.

'That was all, I think, Ruth,' said Cynthia's slow voice.

She had been telling me something and I had not been listening. We were walking round the garden in the mid-morning break.

'Oh yes, thanks,' I said absent-mindedly.

'But it's not true, is it?' she asked.

'True? What isn't true?'

'Why, what I've just been telling you,' she said with feeble protest. 'What they're all saying – that your father went mad and killed someone and had to be put away.'

So that was it. Somebody had got hold of the notion of madness, but since Miss Murry was so obviously sane, it had to be attached to the father of the child.

'Of course it isn't true,' I said with a laugh. 'My father wrote poetry. He was badly wounded in the War and died of wounds. You can tell them that if you like. That is God's truth. Cross my heart. I swear it.' I laughed again at the thought that if Miss Murry's account was correct, this was indeed the truth. My father had been badly wounded during the War, and he had died of wounds.

Cynthia looked relieved. 'Why don't you tell them yourself?'

'Because they are so silly, making up all these stupid stories. Why should I bother to deny them? I've done nothing wrong.'

'Oh, Ruth,' she cried in her sycophantic way, 'you do look splendid when you flash your eyes like that. Just like Clara Bow. And you've got the same coloured hair. I'm sure you're going to be a film star and have lots of admirers.'

I put on an act for her benefit, but all the time I kept telling myself that she was even sillier than Minnie at Miss Greenfield's village school, and asking myself whether I was ever going to have a real friend.

CHAPTER X

TWO DAYS before the end of term I wrote to Miss Murry saying I should like to spend the Christmas holidays with Uncle Matthew. He was lonely and was growing old and I wanted to do something for him in return for his kindness to me. Besides, I continued, it was quiet and peaceful at the cottage and I could get on with my studies in preparation for the university scholarship examination that I was to sit next year. 'I expect you will be having a lot of visitors over Christmas,' I added, 'or perhaps you are going abroad?'

I wanted her to understand that she need not concern herself with me. She sent back a message through the school secretary to the effect that Mr Baines was ill and would not want to be bothered with me, that we would spend

Christmas at home, and that a hired car would be collecting me and my luggage since she was too busy with her own end-of-term activities to collect me herself.

I made my own plans on the assumption that the driver would be the one who was always employed to transport the few girls who, like myself, had no fond parents arriving in limousines to collect their daughters. When the moment came I recognized him with pleasure and relief.

'We're to go round by Littleford,' I said to him in my most superior manner, 'to deliver a parcel to Mr Baines – the gardener, you know. It's not much out of our way.'

'Righto, miss.'

He was a little brown man not unlike Uncle Matthew and he grinned to himself as he put my cases in. I got into the front seat beside him.

'Why are you laughing at me?' I asked as we set off.

'I'm not laughing, miss.'

'But you are,' I insisted. 'Is it because it seems funny for a girl of my age to be giving instructions? Is that it?'

He admitted at last that I did appear to be a very grand young lady.

'But you wouldn't laugh if it was any one of the others,' I said. 'Don't worry. I'm not going to make any complaint about you. I only want to know why I am different. You take it for granted that the others should give instructions. It's only funny when I do it. Why is that, I wonder?'

'Well, miss.' The poor man took a hand off the steering-wheel to tug at his chauffeur's cap. I had made him as puzzled as I was myself. 'Well, miss,' he said at last, 'it's like as if you're acting it, see? Like you don't believe it yourself. You're making fun of it all, see?'

I did indeed see. In fact I had known it all the time but it had never come home to me with quite such force as at this moment. No wonder I could make no real friends at Freelands School, and it was not only my circumstances that were to blame. Had I sheltered modestly under Miss Murry's protection and been suitably unobtrusive, I might have got through my schooldays comfortably enough. At the worst I would have been tolerated, as Cynthia was; at the best I might have found occasional friendly companionship, if not a close friend. It was my own behaviour that had made this impossible. They had all recognized it and reacted to it, even if they had not put it into words. My whole attitude was a constant mocking criticism of their own way of life, and my teasing of Cynthia about her wedding plans was simply the culmination of this process.

I laughed aloud and began to indulge both the driver and myself with a truly virulent take-off of some of the more pompous of the parents whom we had seen greeting their offspring. But it was only to hide the great emptiness that had come over me again when I realized what a useless pretence my whole life at Freelands School had been. My mockery rose to a frenzy as we came near Littleford, and then it suddenly died away completely as we drew up in the lane that led down to the river. How tiny it all looked, even smaller than when I had been there the previous summer : the little white wooden gate, the narrow gravel path, the worn doorstep.

'Just wait a minute,' I said to the driver.

'What about the parcel?' he called after me.

'I'll come back. I want to see how he is first.'

Of course there was no parcel. That was only an excuse. I had come here to stay.

I found him sitting shivering over the fire, his little nut-face more wrinkled than ever and of an unhealthy yellowish colour. There were crumbs on the table and an unwashed

cup and plate, although it was long past breakfast time.
He took a moment or two to recognize me and then he
began to say something about Miss Murry. I interrupted
him, saying that I had brought my luggage and was not
going away again. He tried to speak once more but was
overcome by a fit of coughing that left him gasping. I called
the driver. He looked at Uncle Matthew and shook his
head.

'Ought to be in bed,' he said, 'with a cough like that.'

'Of course he ought,' I cried impatiently. 'He needs
looking after. I'm going to stay with him. I can't leave him
alone. You must bring my things in.'

'But Miss Murry . . .' he began.

'I'll explain to Miss Murry,' I said in a tremendous voice
that filled the little room. I felt very tall – indeed my head
was not very far off the low beam in the ceiling – and I felt
enormously strong and free.

'Look,' I said, 'I'll write her a note. You can take it back
with you. It will save you having to explain to her yourself.'

In the case that contained my school-books I found pen
and paper. I pushed the dirty crockery aside and sat down
at the table.

'Dear Uncle Matthew is very ill,' I wrote, 'and I don't
like to leave him. I'm sure you will understand. He's been
like a father to me. Please try to understand and don't be
angry with me. And don't be angry with the driver. I made
him come.'

I signed it, slipped it into an envelope, and stuck it up.
There was no need to read it through. This incoherent
scrawl would get the message across as clearly as pages of
reasoned self-justification would have done. I am my own
and nobody else's Ruth, it said: if nobody will give me an
identity then I must make my own. I'll choose my home.

I'll choose whom I will love.

The reply, which Mrs Winter brought over later in the day, was very cool.

'Of course you must do what you feel to be your duty. I trust you will give me notice if you do propose to spend any of the holidays at home. I have no intention of going away myself.'

But there was a sting in the tail:

'I understand from my own doctor, whom I requested to examine him, that Mr Baines is seriously ill. Such treatment as is possible has been prescribed and the nurse is paying him regular visits. I do hope, for his sake as well as yours, that you will appreciate that emotional outbursts are in no sense an adequate substitute for correct medical care.'

It hurt me quite a lot before I was able to think it over calmly. Correct medical care, I thought; that's what she gave her own father. But perhaps he might have been all the better for a few emotional outbursts. She is really very cold and hard. All that sympathy when I was a child was only put on; she likes to see herself as perfect, treating everybody exactly as they ought to be treated, but there's nothing behind it. She doesn't really care.

I was very hard myself in my judgment of Miss Murry. In spite of all the rumours, I didn't in my heart believe that she was my mother, and perhaps it was my great disappointment that she was not my mother that made me so very hard on her.

Those last few weeks of Uncle Matthew's life were at the same time the saddest and the happiest weeks that I had ever known. He needed me. The nurse and the neighbours made frequent visits but there was no mistaking the relief on his face when finally the front door was bolted for the night.

'Lot of magpies,' he would mutter, leaning back against the pillows. 'Never could abide women's chatter. Heard too much of it.'

I laughed. 'You chose the wrong job, then, in a girls' school.'

'Ah!' He produced the ghost of a wink. 'Young ladies now. That's a different kettle of fish.'

'You wicked old snob!' I cried. 'You ought to hear the young ladies when the teachers are out of the room. You'd hear more bad language than you've ever heard in your life.'

He shook his head and said 'Ah!' very slowly. He was storing up his breath and saving his strength for his next little story.

'Did I ever tell you about the time I took over the brandy-snap stall at St Giles's Fair?' he asked.

I settled myself to listen. We had brought a bed down into the tiny living-room and there was only just space left to get in and out. If he turned his head to one side he could look out of the window at the line of the hedge that ran along the towing-path and the grey winter sky beyond; if he looked the other way he could see the piano and the fireplace with his old black horsehair chair beside it. Usually I sat on a hard chair by the bed, but sometimes he would doze off in the middle of a story and then I would move over to the horsehair chair and have a little sleep myself, for I seldom stayed in bed at night for more than a couple of hours.

After her initial suspicion of me, the visiting nurse consented to show me how to care for him, and her admission that I wasn't doing too badly was one of the dearest

"I won't be such a hypocrite," she replies, all scornful. "I haven't done anything wrong and I'm not ashamed of anything. We love each other and I don't care who knows it." "Then do it for my sake," begs my lady, "and for the sake of the child, for if anything goes wrong and Julian should not get his freedom – " "Not get his freedom!" she cries, beside herself with fury, "not get his freedom! He'll get his freedom if I have to strangle his wife!" "Hush, hush, Ruth," says Miss Murry, "that isn't the way to hold him. You must control yourself." But she raves and storms about the wife who will not let him go. Daughter of Lady-something-or-other, she was. A real ladyship, not like Miss Murry. It was just my little joke, calling her my lady. "Try to be patient," she said. "Give them time. His wife will come to see that Julian doesn't love her any more. We must hope that she will be generous and let him go." But it was my opinion that this daughter of Lady-something-or-other did love him very dearly, and Miss Murry thought so too.'

He paused to cough. I sat like a statue, praying that nobody would come in and that he would not fall asleep again and that his mind would remain on the track where it was now running.

'Poor Ruth,' he said, moving his head from side to side. 'She didn't understand, for all she was so clever. She didn't know what folks are like. There never was a divorce. He never meant there to be, that's my opinion. He told her he didn't care for his wife but he told his wife a different tale, I'll be bound. He was so good at pretending that you had to believe him even when you knew it could not be true. Except with the baby.'

He fell silent again and there was no sound in the room save for his wheezy breath and the heavy tick of the grandfather clock. And the thumping of my own heart that seemed to want to burst from my chest. I held my hands clenched together between my knees. My lips moved as I silently implored him to go on.

He heaved himself up suddenly, tugging at the bed-clothes, and turned his head right round to look at me. His faded blue eyes were glazed and watery. They seemed to see me and yet not to see me. It was uncanny; I could not bear it; I had to look away.

'It was the baby he loved,' he said. 'That's why he came. Because he wanted to see the baby.'

I looked at him again and saw his face pucker up as if he were about to cry. He picked at the bedclothes and murmured a few inaudible words. And then his voice came out loud and clear and not in the least confused.

'It was all wrong. It could come to no good. But she was so pretty. She was my light of life and it could come to no good.'

He choked on the last word and began to cough, the worst attack I had yet witnessed. I brought the medicines prescribed and propped him high on the pillows and wiped his glistening face. A long time later he took my hand and whispered :

'Thank you, little Ruth. You're a good girl. A good, good girl.'

A week later he died, very peacefully at last after a prolonged and heart-sickening bout of coughing and chok-ing, at about four o'clock in the morning. I closed his eyes and drew the bedcover up to his chin so that nothing was visible save the little dry kernel of a head. Then I leaned back in the black horsehair chair and looked at the glowing coals in the grate. All was quiet and still. The little moans and the scraping breaths were gone for ever and nothing remained but the tick of the grandfather clock.

I must have slept a while, or perhaps my exhaustion had brought hallucinations, for at one time there appeared an elderly lady in the chair opposite me, and a small girl sitting on a tuffet in front of the fire, with her head propped in her hands and a book on her knees. She seemed to be very frightened for some reason or other and I wanted to comfort her and say: Don't be afraid; there's kindness and love; there's nothing to fear.

But a big lump of coal suddenly fell apart with a sharp crackle and made me start, and when I sat up and looked around me there was nobody else there and I was very cold. I got up and went down the stone passage to the scullery and made tea. Then I returned to the fire and wrapped a rug round myself and sat perfectly still until the first faint chirpings of sparrows and the lightening greyness in the square of the window told me that a new day had dawned.

CHAPTER XI

I SAID goodbye to him then, during those still hours of the night. The next day the cottage became a public place, with the nurse and the doctor and the neighbours and the vicar and Uncle Matthew's nephew who lived in London and had visited him once during the last week of his illness. They were all kind to me but I embarrassed them. I had played my part and there was no place for me now. My little dream of becoming a part of the village community melted away like snow in spring. Minnie would hate it if I were

to trip about the teashop with her; Miss Greenfield would
be uncomfortable if I were to try to teach the little ones
at the far end of the long schoolroom.

So I packed up my belongings and drove away with Miss
Murry after the funeral, on a raw wet February day. She
looked tired and old and was very silent, and when we got
to Rivermead it seemed to me that the whole house had
lost its elegant crispness and sparkle. Her cousin, who was
staying with her, whispered to me that it was 'something
to do with her age'.

I wanted to apologize for my difficult behaviour but
there was no way in which we could make contact. She
seemed to have lost all interest in everything. Even when
I said I didn't want to go back to Freelands School she
made little protest. Arrangements were made for me to
attend some lectures and have some private tuition, and
now and then she would conscientiously inquire how my
studies were going. I was always glad, however, when Sunday was over and she returned to her duties at St Margaret's
School, for I felt much less lonely when Mrs Winter and I
were by ourselves in the house than I did when its owner
was present.

Often I was completely alone, for Mrs Winter liked to
make shopping excursions into Oxford and go on to see
her friends in Headington, and on such occasions I would
wander about the rooms and out into the garden, saying
to myself : It all happened here; in this place my father and
mother loved guiltily and I came into being. Sometimes
I would open up the bureau and turn over the piles of letters
and household bills that Miss Murry had kept there since
her father's death, but it was only a desultory action and I
did not really expect to find any documents that would

throw light on my own past. Anything of real importance
would be kept in her study at St Margaret's School, where
she dealt with her correspondence with the help of the
school secretary.

But even if I had found myself alone and uninterrupted
in her school study, I doubt whether I would have taken
any action. I craved to know the truth and at the same time
I was terrified by the prospect of learning it from a cold,
impersonal source. It was as if I was split into two. There
was myself as branded by the law and public opinion and
even up to a point by Miss Murry herself : illegitimate child
of a criminally lunatic mother, a social problem, a name in
official files, a bit of human wreckage on which to exercise
the social conscience. This was the self I would see in cruel
loveless print if ever I had a sight of the documents in the
case. And then there was the other Ruth, the Ruth whom
I felt myself to be. The one who had crouched behind the
bushes long ago and been shocked into a maturity beyond
her years by the sudden vision of the branded self; the Ruth
who loved to read poetry and for whom the vast free world
of the imagination was always within easy reach; the Ruth
who had wished for nothing else in the world than to sit
at the bedside of an old man dying.

But there were other sick people in the world; there
might be a place for the second Ruth. Why should I not
go along to the local cottage hospital, who were always
appealing for help, and try in the service of others to forget
my branded self?

I cycled over to Littleford to see the district nurse who
had showed me how to look after Uncle Matthew, and
borrowed some booklets from her about training facilities.
The big teaching hospitals, I discovered, would not take a

girl for training until she was twenty-one, but some of the smaller ones would now take them at eighteen. So in a few months' time I should be old enough to be a probationer nurse at a cottage hospital. Filled with the heady notion of myself as a ministering angel, and fortified by the much less innocent idea that I should be revenging myself on Miss Murry by abandoning my academic career, I presented myself at the cottage hospital and asked to see the matron.

She listened amicably when I told her that I wanted to be a nurse.

'Do your parents approve of your taking this step?' she asked.

It came as a curious little shock, not entirely unpleasant, to realize that here was an older person, someone in authority, who knew nothing of my history and circumstances. For a moment I was tempted to invent a home and background according to my own prescription, but that would ruin my chances at once, and my desire to be a nurse was genuine, even if it sprang partly from such an unworthy motive. I therefore replied that I had no parents, only a guardian.

'And what does he think of it?' asked the matron.

It seemed to me that the expression on her face had changed and that her manner was not quite so encouraging as before.

'Actually it's a she,' I replied. 'Miss Annette Murry, headmistress of St Margaret's School in Oxford. You may have heard of her. She is quite well known. She writes books on teaching methods and gives lectures to university students.'

The slight coolness that I had perhaps imagined disappeared from the matron's face. Evidently orphans were somewhat suspect unless vouched for by irreproachable citizens like Miss Murry. But the bitterness that was welling up within me again did not so easily disperse, and I had to struggle for calm as I answered her subsequent questions. My mother had been a pupil at the school, I said, and my father was killed in the War. There were no close relatives left on either side and it had been arranged that Miss Murry should be my guardian; it had all taken place when I was very young and I had known no other home.

I thought of Uncle Matthew even as I spoke these words and hated myself for the lie; hated Miss Murry too, and the matron, and everyone and everything that had contributed to my feeling that I had to lie if I was to have a chance to help others in the way I wished.

'I'll tell you a little more about the training scheme,' said the matron, 'and I'll give you an application form for you to show Miss Murry when you talk it all over with her. She will no doubt want to get in touch with me herself. We shall want references, of course. Somebody from your own school would be suitable, and another person of professional standing who knows you well. And you will need to have a medical examination. And we shall want your birth certificate – as evidence of age, you know.'

Even before this final blow I had realized that my scheme was hopeless. The matron knew nothing of my branded self, but every word she spoke was making it more and more clear that the real Ruth had not the slightest chance of training as a nurse because the branded Ruth would have to be revealed, and once revealed would stand inexorably in the way. Put helpless patients into the hands of a girl with such an inheritance! The idea was unthinkable. There was no hope unless Miss Murry would consent to lie about my parentage, and even if we had not been as estranged as we now were, I could not have asked her to do this.

I took the paper from the matron and stretched my lips into an artificial smile as I thanked her.

'Do I need to let you know if I decide not to apply?' I asked.

'Well, no. This is only a preliminary inquiry. But of course I hope that you will decide to go ahead.'

It seemed to me that she had seen right into my thoughts and knew everything about me and that her smile was as false as my own. I got out of the building somehow and found my bicycle and rode slowly home. At first I was utterly wretched, telling myself that it was my fate to be frustrated at every turn and that I had no chance of making my way in life with such a millstone round my neck. But after a while I was able to think more clearly, and I remembered that in fact I was being coached to take my place among the privileged few at Oxford University, so it was hardly fair to complain that I was being given no chance in life.

But it was all Miss Murry's doing. She had formed me, made me acceptable at my school and among her friends by glossing over the truth, twisting things round so that I appeared to be different from what I was. She was very good at such character-editing, as well I knew from the times when she insisted on presenting me as 'little Ruth'. So it looked as if there was yet a third Ruth, midway between the branded one and the real one : the girl who was the creation of Miss Annette Murry.

Suddenly it all became so plain to me that I nearly fell off my bicycle and had to stop for a moment, with one foot on the grassy bank propping myself up, and the other foot kicking at the pedal. Of course I was sulky and rebellious and longing to escape, but the answer was not to run away, as I had tried to do when I was a child, but to bring all three Ruths together, make them come to terms with each other, and then at last I should be able to face whatever life had in store. The real Ruth would be all right, given the chance, and Miss Murry's version would be firmly put in her place as time went on, but it was the branded one who was the trouble and who was going to be more of a nuisance the older I grew. Parentage, birth certificates, next-of-kin – all these obstacles were going to crop up again and again throughout my life. I had got to dig out and piece together the branded Ruth, every little bit of her, without prejudice and without emotion, as if I were an archaeologist re-creating an antique vase from its shattered fragments; there was to be no more shrinking from cold print, no more dramatizing myself as a mysterious figure. I would draw up a list of clues as they did in the detective stories, and plan out a line of campaign.

How cowardly I had become, I thought as I pedalled excitedly away, to have sheltered behind Miss Murry's Ruth all these years. I had been silly and rash as a child, but at least I had had more courage. I really had tried to find out. I put my bicycle away in the garage and let myself into the house very quietly, hoping that Mrs Winter would not hear me and that I could go up to my room unnoticed. But I had to contain my impatience and my excitement because she came into the hall at the same moment as I did and dragged me off to an early lunch before she caught the bus into Oxford. The agitations of the morning had taken away my usually healthy appetite. I managed the lamb chop but stuck on the vegetables and Mrs Winter remarked on it.

'Though I don't think much of this cabbage,' she added. 'Our garden produce hasn't been the same since Mr Baines was taken from us.'

'You can't blame the new man for the winter vegetables,' I retorted. 'They were already in when he came.'

She took my plate away with an irritable little jerk and went to fetch the pudding. Even my relations with Mrs Winter had deteriorated since my weeks at Littleford. We had previously got on very happily, for I knew instinctively that I was not to talk to her about my parents and that Miss Murry would have told her whatever story she needed to know. Our conversation had been confined to food and clothes and film stars, for like the girls at Freelands School she was an avid cinema-goer. We also gossiped about Miss Murry's visitors, but never about Miss Murry herself. It was distressing to feel no longer at ease with Mrs Winter, but I could see no way to get back to our former footing.

'Perhaps I'd better not go out,' she said as she watched me pushing a piece of my favourite lemon sponge around the plate. 'You don't look at all well to me and Miss Murry won't be home till after six.'

I told her that I had been to see the district nurse who had looked after Mr Baines and had been given two huge slices of cake and that was why I wasn't hungry. Actually my visit had been the day before, but it was easier to tell a tale with some truth in it than to invent one completely. Mrs Winter was annoyed that I had not mentioned this earlier, but at least she stopped worrying about my health. I helped her clear up and then went up to my bedroom and stood at the window to watch her walk down the drive.

As soon as she had disappeared behind the yew hedge I opened the ebony box where I kept precious things like a signed copy of an article written by the English mistress at school, and a few trinkets given to me by Miss Murry's friends, and a fountain pen from Professor West that was

used only for special occasions like making a fair copy of a
poem I had written. I put these to one side and came across
Uncle Matthew's watch that used to hang on a chain from
his waistcoat. Underneath it was the faded photograph of
himself and his mates setting up their tent on the island in
the river, and below that again, at the bottom of the box,
were the pictures of my father and mother that Miss Murry
had given to me when she told me of my mother's death.

I had scarcely looked at them since. I had let my fears
and my imagination take over. Even during my heart-
searchings following my big quarrel with Miss Murry I had
not thought to refer to the photographs; even after Uncle
Matthew died and I had added his watch to my treasures,
I had not cared to do more than glance at the pictures. The
Julian and Ruth about whom Uncle Matthew had spoken
still belonged to my fantasy, but I was determined to look
at the reality now.

There was one framed portrait and two snapshots. I laid
them side by side on the dressing-table. The picture of Ruth
my mother looked as if it had been taken in her late teens.
It was stiff and posed. Her hair was piled up on top of her
head, perhaps for the first time in her life, and her neck and
shoulders were swathed in lace. There was a sweet sickly
smile on her lips that was at odds with the eyes, which held
no laughter but looked out with a strange half-frightened,
half-menacing expression from under dark brows. She
obviously disliked the camera; no wonder she had been no
good as an actress.

The snapshot of Ruth showed her sitting in a punt. Only
half the boat was visible and presumably the other occupant
had been deliberately left out of the picture. My father,
perhaps? At any rate the wooden wall of the boathouse was
unmistakable to the left of the picture, and so was the

background of willow-trees on the opposite bank of the river. It had been taken from the lawn by somebody standing a few feet from the water's edge. Ruth looked happy here. She had on a simple dress of some striped material; her hair was piled high but wisps of it were escaping down her neck and she was waving a paddle in the air as if it were a tennis racket. It looked as if somebody had just made a joke and caught her in gay and uninhibited response.

She was vital and beautiful; she was the girl whom Uncle Matthew and old Mr Murry had loved. She was their Ruth as I was Miss Murry's Ruth. But she too had had another self – the dark and menacing Ruth whom the old men had only glimpsed but whom Miss Murry must have known well. The Ruth, above all, whom Julian had known in addition to the gay and brilliant girl he loved; the Ruth who had been the death of him.

My studied coolness faltered as I turned to the picture of my father. It was not a snapshot, as I had at first thought, but a half-length portrait, a photographer's proof copy perhaps, or a finished portrait denied the dignity of glass and gilt frame because my mother had no legal right to its possession. It must have been tucked away among her treasures as it was now hidden among my own, a furtive, guilty joy.

I looked with fearful fascination at the image of this man who was the cause of my being, and Uncle Matthew's words came back to me : he was so clever at pretending, but he really did love the baby. I looked first at the uniform – a captain's. And then I looked at the face and found myself recoiling as if I had received a physical shock, so clearly and mockingly did the dark eyes look up at me. And there was a sardonic twist to the mouth too. It was the cruelty that hit me first and only after that did I see how handsome he was. He had done great harm; he had caused much unhappiness. He had deceived his wife and no doubt other women too, and in the end he had driven my poor mother right out of her mind with despair so that she had destroyed both him and herself, but his had been a quick and easy end while she had suffered years of living death. He had a terrible lot to answer for.

But he had truly loved the baby.

I gulped back rising tears. You never knew this man Julian, I told myself firmly; it is Uncle Matthew for whom you are mourning now. But I must have known him, I protested; if he loved the baby then the baby must have known him, the baby must have loved him. And in any case she was no longer a baby when he died; she was a child of six, a child who was shortly to go through an experience so shattering that it blotted out nearly all the earlier memories and left only a few flashes of vision and a great all-embracing fear.

The tears sprang again. I put my hand over the photograph and laid my forehead upon it. My hand was cold and shaking but my face was burning as if with fever. I banged my head against the back of my hand again and again. My father who must have loved me, I whispered, and I can't even remember.

After a while I became a little calmer and was once more able to look at the photograph. So much for my scientific search for truth, I said aloud, addressing it: yes, you may well sneer at me, but I can be mocking too, I can make people fear me; you ought to have seen me with some of the girls at school; I wish I could tell you, I wish I could talk to you, I wish I could remember how you must have talked to me.

I propped my head in my hands and stared at the face

and bit my lips in concentration. There must be something buried there beneath the surface. Other memories had successfully broken the barrier. I knew the sense of my mother's presence; I knew the books and the big window and the scent of roses in Miss Murry's room. I knew the feel of hospital. They had put me there to recover from the severe shock of nearly drowning, so Miss Murry had reluctantly told me. And I knew the boathouse and the willow-branch and myself in the water.

Then why did I not know my father? Because I had been deliberately discouraged from remembering, I told myself angrily. I would drag the names of his relatives and his wife's relatives from Miss Murry, I decided, and I would go and see them. Nothing should shake me in that resolve. But meanwhile I yearned for one little flicker of recognition, just the least hint that this dark face that looked up at me was so closely connected with myself.

Sometimes I thought I knew it and sometimes I thought I was building on my imagination alone. But what did emerge clearly from my deep questioning was the memory of a conversation that I had overheard in Miss Murry's drawing-room, about a year ago, before Mr Murry died and Professor West went to America. They had been talking about the treatment of shell-shocked soldiers just after the War, and about a doctor – an Austrian, I think they said – who believed that people could only recover from the loss of memory brought on by shock if they were able to bring back to mind the thing that had shocked them. Otherwise all the horror of the experience stayed festering away in their minds and made them ill. At that point Miss Murry had asked me to fetch a book for her that she had left in her bedroom, and when I returned with it they were talking about something else. I had not suspected anything at the

time because she often sent me on little errands, but now
I began to wonder. Had this been yet another instance of
her determination to mould me into the Ruth she wanted
me to be?

CHAPTER XII

SOME WAY to bring back the memory. Wasn't that just what
I needed myself, and wasn't that just what Miss Murry
didn't want me to know about? They had called it something – something to do with the mind, the psyche. Psycho-
analysis. It suddenly came back to me. Why, I had even
asked Miss Murry about it, not immediately after that
particular conversation but a little later on. The English
teacher at school had mentioned it. I could even remember
Miss Murry's reply. Conscientious but not encouraging.
It would be against her principles to say outright : 'Don't
read this book,' but she had very cleverly managed to
imply that it would not interest me, that it was a new
medical technique but so far completely unproved and that
doctors were in disagreement themselves about it. She had
linked it up with other developments in medicine – the
search for a drug to treat tuberculosis, for example – and
had left me with the overwhelming impression that psycho-
analysis could have no relevance or interest for a lay person.
And then, as far as I could recollect, she had slid neatly
back to Eliot's new volume of poetry.

Yes, Julian, I said to the picture, she took me in good
and proper. Very skilful at diverting my thoughts into safe
channels, very shrewd is my dear guardian Nan.

I got up from the dressing-table and went downstairs to

the drawing-room. Here was a clue that I could follow up
straight away, that had indeed been under my eyes for
months without my realizing it. I opened the glass doors of
the bureau bookcase and ran my hand along the lowest
shelf. Here were Miss Murry's most recent acquisitions. She
read reviews and made notes when her guests talked and
kept up with all the newest ideas. If there was anything to
find I would find it here. Unless she had taken the books
to her study at St Margaret's to be out of my reach. But I
did not think she would do that, for she would scorn such
crude methods of concealment. To guide and control my
mind, to turn me into her Ruth, to rely on the strength of
her own intellect and personality – this was her way.

A couple of titles seemed to me to be relevant and I was
just about to take the books from the shelf when the front
doorbell rang. I went to answer it, my mind still running
on the idea of recovering forgotten memories, and for a
second or two I did not recognize the tall man in horn-
rimmed glasses who stood at the door, awkwardly clutching
a large box full of books.

'Professor West!' I cried at last. He looked different,
younger and not so thin as when I had last seen him. Or
perhaps it was I who had changed. 'Miss Murry isn't here,'
I said.

'I know,' he replied. 'She's on the way, coming home via
Abingdon. They told me so at school.'

My little flash of joyful surprise vanished at these words:
I wanted him to myself; I didn't want Miss Murry to
come. He staggered into the hall with the books and I
moved a vase of daffodils aside so that he could put them
on the table.

'Do you want to wait to see her?' I asked.

'That was part of the idea.' He stretched his arms gratefully after dumping the books. 'They will write so much,
these Americans. Nothing under a thousand pages is worthy
of publication. However, I've brought back all she asked
for. God knows when she'll have the time to read them.'

Suddenly I was happy again. 'D'you want some tea?' I
asked. 'I was just going to make it for myself.'

'Then I will help you. Do you know,' he went on as I
led the way to the kitchen, 'I've never penetrated into
the domestic offices in this establishment. How very
superior. But then I might have guessed that it would be
Scandinavian white wood. Always have to have the very
latest, don't we?'

'Actually,' I said, 'I don't much like it. It looks like a
clinic. I'd rather have the old black grate and stone hearth
at my uncle's in Littleford.'

I caught my breath the moment I had spoken, remembering that Uncle Matthew was no longer there. Professor West
ignored my gasp and picked up the tray.

'In the sitting-room,' I said. I had forgotten that I had
left open the glass door of the bookcase. Of course he went
straight to it as soon as he had set down the tray.

'What's the current craze?' he asked. 'It was all T. S.
Eliot when I last saw you.'

'Do you know anything about psycho-analysis?' I asked
on a sudden impulse as I poured out his tea.

He gave a groan. 'Oh no, Ruth. Not that. I've just come
from a New York full of it. It's all the rage, like yo-yo.
Freud in ten easy lessons and then, oh boy, you're free –
free of all inhibitions and repressions and what-have-you.
It's a menace. Honest it is. A terrifying woman at a literary
party came up to me and fixed me with an Ancient

Mariner's eye and held on to my coat and told me I'd been avoiding her all evening because as a child I had unconsciously wanted to murder my mother. I hadn't, you know. My mother died when I was born. But I had wanted to avoid the lady. She had a voice like chalk squeaking on the blackboard. Oh, how glad I am to be home!'

I laughed and he told me more about New York. And then he said, in the same excited, tumbling voice, which I knew was yet perfectly serious: 'Psycho-analysis. The best introduction is that little book by Evelyn Briggs. Very few books are either sane or intelligible, but this one miraculously manages to be both. It's written by a lady doctor. Your guardian will have it, I expect. She'd never miss out on a craze of this magnitude. Didn't I see a copy on the shelf?'

He was up again, knocking against a small table so that it shook and the Swedish glassware standing on it wobbled perilously. He was himself rather a menace, though not in the same way as the American lady, in a drawing-room.

'Here it is,' he cried. And then his tone instantly changed when he saw my face. 'But perhaps you would rather not take her copy, perhaps you don't want to discuss the topic with her. In that case I will lend you my own copy.'

How had he read my thoughts so quickly? I was amazed, delighted, and finally resolved, in rapid succession over a matter of seconds. What a wonderful prospect, Professor West and myself in league together against Miss Murry! But it would not do.

'Thanks,' I said calmly, 'but I would rather borrow her copy. After all, she is my guardian and I wouldn't like her to think I'm going behind her back.'

It came out as intolerably priggish and insincere, although I believed myself to have spoken from genuine feelings of loyalty.

'You're quite right, Ruth,' he said, 'my mistake,' and then he switched over, very obviously this time, to his own recent experiences.

I was wretchedly unhappy and had none of the quiet satisfaction that surely ought to result from temptation successfully resisted. With all my heart I wished my words unsaid, wished myself now sitting near him on the low stool, as once I had sat on the grass by Miss Murry's deckchair and made daisy chains, wished myself now pouring out all the doubts and fears that I had hugged to myself for so long, and my more recent hopes and resolutions, testing their strength and truth against this sparkling mind that understood so quickly and so well.

'You're not looking too bright, Ruth,' he said, breaking off in the middle of an anecdote. 'Is there anything the matter? Is there anything I can do?'

'Uncle Matthew died,' I murmured. 'I miss him rather. He was the first person I can remember. Really remember, I ought to say. I do have some sort of impressions about my mother, and some early impressions about Miss Murry too, but they are very confused and have got all mixed up with her as I have known her since I came back from Littleford.'

'Yes, of course,' he said. 'Tell me about Mr Baines. When did he die? I'm very sorry to hear it.'

So it all came out easily after all, or most of it, without any feeling of guilt or disloyalty on my part. He knew the framework of my history, of course, but I re-told it now with myself inside the frame, repeating the rumour that Miss Murry was my mother, but leaving out my suspicion that she had never told me the full truth about my parents.

'She thinks it best that I should not get in touch with any of my parents' relatives or with anybody who knew them,' was all I said. 'I can see why she thinks so, in a way, but

H

I can't help wanting to, all the same. Could you?'

'Good heavens, no. Any mystery about my origins and I'd have been on to it like a ferret the moment I could move and speak. I think you've been remarkably patient and restrained.'

'But there's probably no mystery,' I said, feeling dampened rather than elated by his approval. 'I'm probably imagining everything. I don't suppose there is anything to know other than what she has told me and if I ever did find anyone related to my mother or father they would probably know nothing about it or not want to talk to me if they did. The only thing I can't help regretting is that I was never allowed to go and see my mother before she died. I think Miss Murry ought to have taken me, don't you?'

'Do you?' He looked at me for a moment or two with an expression that I could not fathom. 'Do you think that would have been wise?'

'Wise!' I cried. 'What's being wise got to do with it? It's how I felt. Wouldn't you have wanted to go in my place? Wouldn't you? Wouldn't you?'

He jumped up from his chair and once again the Swedish glasses rocked and rattled. 'Yes, I should have wanted to,' he said, pacing about the room, frowning, pulling faces, and glaring at me. 'But I don't know,' he said at last, sitting down again, 'I don't know whether it would have been for the best.'

There was something in the quality of his agitation that made me suspicious and sent my questing mind wildly off on a new tack.

'There's something you know!' I cried. 'She's told you something that she hasn't told me. You've got to tell me, you must. Can't you see how I feel, not knowing?'

I caught hold of his arm with both my hands and moved it roughly backwards and forwards on the arm of his chair.

'You must tell me what she told you,' I said again. 'I can't live like this, questioning everything. It's killing me. I must know who I am, I must, I must!'

He put his hand over both of mine and turned to face my upturned face and said in a voice of great kindness, all the sweeter for being so unlike his usual brusque and jerky tones : 'Dear Ruth. I want nothing but to help you. Do you remember when I pulled you off the bank on the towpath?'

'Yes,' I replied. 'I remember it all. Every single detail. As clear as can be.'

'You looked very lost and wild and unchildlike. It interested me but it alarmed me too. I was very anxious about you. But you very cleverly manoeuvred me into bringing you to Miss Murry's school instead of taking you back to Mr Baines's cottage.'

I felt myself changing colour as he said this, but didn't mind him seeing it.

'Oh,' I said, 'did you realize that I was trying to make you do that?'

'Not at the time. I thought you were really a little girl lost from the rest of the party, but later on I began to suspect. Why didn't you want to go back to Littleford? Why did you run away from Mr Baines when you were so fond of him?'

'Because I had overheard,' I began, and then had to stop to control my voice. I had never told anyone, not even Miss Murry, exactly what had happened on that bright summer day so many years ago. It was sharply painful to remember and, as always, talking about it seemed at first to make it feel worse.

He held my hands and looked at me with great compassion and waited. It was just then I thought I heard a footstep on the gravel path outside the french windows, but the moment was so precious that I could not bear to turn round or draw away.

'I overheard Mrs Baines complaining to a visitor about having had to take me in,' I said firmly. 'Miss Murry didn't know what to do with me after my mother shot my father and she thought it would be best if I was brought up in different surroundings with nothing to remind me of my past life. Mrs Baines didn't know the full story but she was afraid that I had inherited criminal tendencies and that I might turn into a criminal myself.'

I stopped abruptly. I had been going to add that I thought Miss Murry had been very cruel to turn me out of my familiar surroundings and put me away in a little village as if I was a shameful secret, but it suddenly occurred to me that this might show me up in a somewhat childish and self-pitying light. And equally suddenly I knew it was tremendously important that he should no longer look on me as Miss Murry's little Ruth. Here was my chance to establish myself with him as the real Ruth, and there wasn't much time left, because she might come back at any moment.

'Mrs Baines was not particularly bright, nor particularly good with children,' I said in an affected drawl. It seemed to me that his lips twitched as if he was trying not to smile, but he said seriously enough : 'And what do you think about it yourself ? Do you think that you are going to turn into a criminal ?'

I shook my head. 'Not now,' I said.

I wanted him to kiss me, hold me, love me like the adult I now felt myself to be. I was trying to make it happen, as I had willed things to happen all those years ago. I was very strong and was going to conquer. I had hoodwinked stupid people often enough; this time I was going to win over a clever man.

We stared at each other for a few moments and then I realized that he was silently laughing, not making fun of me, but with sheer pleasure.

'I don't know anything about your having inherited criminal tendencies, my dear Ruth,' he said, 'but you have certainly acquired some seductive tendencies from somewhere. Very powerful indeed. They need careful handling.'

I laughed with him and exclaimed : 'Good show ! I hoped I had,' and at that moment we both became aware that Miss Murry must have been standing in the open doorway of the sitting-room for a few seconds at least. We both got up, looking rather guilty. She behaved admirably.

'Hullo, Nick,' she said. 'Welcome back. I can't say, "What a surprise," because they told me at school that you had called in. Actually I was still there – I was over in the other house. But in any case I wanted the books brought here. You must have gone to a lot of trouble to get them and I very much appreciate it. Ruth has made tea, I see. Will it run to another cup ?'

She looked at me in calm and friendly inquiry and I felt ashamed, as if I had been slandering her behind her back.

'I'll make you some more,' I said. 'You must be tired.'

'Thank you, my dear. That would be very nice.'

She sank into a chair, looking strained and exhausted in spite of all her poise. And in spite of my own agitation I noticed that she had not called me 'child' and had not spoken to me in a condescending voice, as she had always done before Professor West went away.

I got up, stepped over the two back supports that were slotted into the sides of the punt, and made my way to the sloping end from which Professor West had showed me how to use the pole. A paddle was lying there and I worked the boat round with it until it knocked against the side of the boathouse next to the big willow-tree with the drooping branches that were lapped by the wash when a river steamer passed by. It was too early in the year for the steamers, but the spring current was running very quickly, swirling round the bend of the river and making little waves.

Uncle Matthew had wanted to cut back the tree because it was in the way but Miss Murry had forbidden him to do so. She seldom went on the river herself, but her guests frequently did, and it was out of character for her to put them to inconvenience. She must have some superstitious feeling about the place, to let it remain exactly as it had been when my father died there. If she had really wanted to forget, and wanted me to forget, then she would have had the little wooden hut pulled down and replaced by a structure that held no memories. But here were the very wooden planks, the very same branches, the same little boats. For all I knew, those shabby red cushions now lying folded on the platform were the very ones on to which my father's life blood had drained away.

I put down the paddle, sprawled on the slats at the bottom of the punt, and held it in position by gripping the willow branch. It felt damp and scratchy. My fingers touched a loose tag of bark and automatically began to pull at it. Memory stirred and flared up like a rocket : myself crouching in the bushes behind Uncle Matthew's cottage, tearing the bark away from a branch. I had run away from the others because I could not bear to see them all happy together and myself as the outsider. And it was just the same now. Miss Murry and Professor West together and no place for me.

My fingers were becoming cold and stiff from holding the boat back against the current. It was growing dark. There was not a human creature in sight and no sound save the rustling of small wild creatures in last year's withered undergrowth and the little plops as the running water released loose pieces of gravel from the overhanging bank. There was nothing here to fear and yet my heart was racing and my hands on the willow branch were slackening their grip.

But what does it matter if you do let go, I told myself : the boat is tied up, it will float round with the stream, and you can walk along to the other end of it and step up on to the platform and out of the door and back to the house. And even if the rope should come untied and the boat drift away, yet you have a paddle and you know how to use it. I spoke aloud, furious with myself. But still the panic struck and struck again, freezing me, draining all strength. There had been nothing as bad since the nightmare in childhood. And there was no one to run to. I was paralysed, without the power or the will to move.

My hands slipped at last and the punt swung round and I lay there on the damp wooden slats shivering and moaning and gasping for breath. There was a little bump as we hit the rowing-boat moored alongside and then all movement stopped. My breathing eased. I dared to turn over and prop myself on my hands and look back into the gloom of the little wooden shelter, half-expecting to see the face of the nightmare. But all the noise and fury of screaming voices that had been splitting my brain apart died away and there was nothing but the dark damp wood and the sense, more than the sound, of lapping water.

I crawled to the centre of the boat and fell against the back-rest. It felt hard against my shoulders but it was solid and real and it brought me peace.

CHAPTER XIII

PNEUMONIA AT that time had not yet lost its gravest terrors, but was still a long, slow, painful and alarming business. I had never been really well since Uncle Matthew's death, and the hours of lying shivering on damp boards had certainly not increased my resistance to a serious illness. Worst of all, I was completely lacking in the will to recover. There was relief when the worst of the fever was over and I could see only the yellow eiderdown and the white cupboard opposite the end of my bed instead of all the kaleidoscopic visions of delirium, but no sight or sound could catch my interest, no thoughts hold within them the seeds of a possible future. I turned my head and watched the clouds move across the rectangle of the window and I wished I could merge with them and dissolve away, as once long ago I had wanted to melt into my reflection in the river.

There were red tulips on the window-ledge, and on a table by my bed there were books and magazines and a chess-set and packs of cards and jigsaw puzzles, and fruit and chocolate and every conceivable object that Miss Murry and her friends and Uncle Matthew's friends and my former school-fellows and teachers had been able to think of to bring comfort to a sickroom. I was being ill in grand style.

I told Professor West so when he arrived with a bowl of hyacinths for which there was no room on the table.

'Would it make you feel better to be put up in the attic and fed on bread and water?' he asked. 'Or dumped into hospital and left strictly alor.e? I dare say it could be arranged for you to be ill in poor style if that's what you really want.'

I tried hard to smile because he always tried so hard to divert me.

'You ought not to approve of all this luxury,' I said, 'a good socialist like you.'

But he only looked worried. 'I wish I could think of something that would really help,' he said.

'There's nothing to help. I just want to be dead.'

'Yes, I know.'

'That's more than Dr Wilkinson does. I'd never dare say so to him. Or to Nan, for that matter.'

'No. Better not. You do realize that it is only a phase, don't you? It will pass.'

'I suppose so,' I said indifferently, wishing he would depart so that I could once more blend myself into the sky. But he got up and began to shift things about on the table, making rather a noise about it and blocking my view of the window.

'The Briggs book!' he exclaimed. 'What a girl you are. Are you trying to enliven your convalescence by studying psycho-analysis?'

'Why not? I'm quite capable of understanding the theory of it. I don't have to go back to reading *Little Women* just because I've had pneumonia.'

'Attagirl! That's the spirit. There's life in you yet, I see. I will therefore remove this pile of *Silver Screen* magazines that someone has had the temerity to leave here and replace it with *Brave New World* and *Jude the Obscure* and a few of Dorothy Sayers's books for light relief. And next time I come I shall expect you to be able to answer questions intelligently and to give me (a) a short summary of Freud's theory of dreams, (b) your considered opinion on whether Aldous Huxley is being unduly pessimistic about our civilization, and (c) your views on Hardy's treatment of the so-called New Woman. And if you can't do this next time I come I shall return every afternoon until you can.' He picked up the pile of film magazines. 'I'll take these back to college. The porter has a wife and daughter who will be very pleased to have them. There's no need to waste good newsprint just because you and I happen to be superior people, is there? I'm off now. And you get down to your reading. I mean it. I'm warning you.'

He kept to his word and bullied me with university examination questions until my head was bursting and I could scarcely see, but from that day forward I began to recover.

I refused to work for university entrance, though, and on this matter Professor West sided with Miss Murry against me. They had drawn very close together during my illness and he spent many weekends and the whole of the Easter vacation with us. Sometimes when we sat over a meal in family intimacy, the three of us, so near yet not related, I was surprised and frightened by the violence of my jealousy, and it was all I could do not to rise from the table and run away, leaving them to the sort of tête-à-tête that they must have enjoyed while I lay in bed. Hour after hour they must have spent together, discussing literature and politics and art, no doubt, but also, I felt equally sure, talking endlessly about what was to be done with me.

It was very hard to bear, not because I suspected that

Miss Murry was still trying to make a child of me, but because I knew she was not. She was her old self again, calm, poised, and always in the right. She seemed to have come to terms with growing old and was no longer fighting back the years, and for all the greying hair and wrinkling skin she was a more dangerous rival than she had been as the strained emotional woman of the previous months. Even my young inexperience was wise enough to know that, and my feelings lent me perception, for I had by now come to love Professor West very dearly – more than I had ever loved Uncle Matthew, more than I had loved Miss Murry in the years before I began seriously to mistrust her. It was not just the admiration of a girl of seventeen for an older man : that was only a minor part of it. It was all the love that had ever been in me and that had never found an object. He was father and mother, brother and sister, teacher, lover and friend. Every possible relationship, every possible variety of human love, came together in my feelings for him.

And yet I had to share him with Miss Murry.

'When are you going to get married?' I asked him one day when the warm weather had come and we were all three sitting on the lawn. He had been telling us about the small house in North Oxford that he had recently bought, and about his plans to move out of his rooms in college within the next few weeks, and this had given me my cue. 'Isn't it time that you did?' I insisted.

It was intended as a joking remark with a little bit of spite in it, but something went wrong with my voice and my manner and it sounded simply impertinent. I saw a look pass between him and my guardian and at that moment I knew what it was to feel like murder.

'Or are you suffering from unrequited love?' I said, still

in the bitter, aggressive voice, the words coming out before
I could stop them.

'I don't think, perhaps, Ruth . . .' began Miss Murry
tentatively, but he interrupted her :

'I am not thinking of getting married and I am not
suffering from unrequited love. There is no secret about it.
A few years ago your suppositions would have had some
basis in fact. She was an opera-singer – quite a well-known
one. She couldn't see herself fitting into academic circles
and broke off the engagement. All very tragic and romantic.
I'm sure your busy imagination can fill out the story for
itself, Ruth. You don't want me to go into detail, do you?'

I turned my head aside and tugged at the grass. I could
not speak. I was in a turmoil of love and hate and pain
and shame. I heard the sound of movement and glanced
round to see Miss Murry disappearing into the house.
Professor West had slid out of his deckchair on to the grass
beside me. His brown eyes surveyed me dispassionately
through the big lenses.

'Well, what are we going to do?' he asked.

'What d'you mean?'

I tugged at the grass yet more frantically.

'What are *you* going to do, I should have said,' he replied.
'You won't go to college. You turn down every other
suggestion that is put to you. Do you propose to stay here
indefinitely as a lady of leisure? Or have you got social
ambitions? Do you want to join the brigade of debs and
be suitably groomed to be launched into the marriage
market of the London season? Is that your ambition?'

'Oh shut up!' I screamed.

He was silent.

'I am shutting up as requested,' he said after a while.
'It's up to you now.'

There was another silence. This time I was the one to break it.

'Anyway, it's nothing to do with you. You're not my guardian.'

'Very true.'

He leaned back, propping himself on one elbow, and continued to study me.

'I suppose she asked you to talk to me,' I said.

'No. I offered to.'

'Why?'

He did not answer.

'I suppose she's afraid to tackle me herself,' I went on.

'You are not always very approachable, Ruth,' he said in a solemn voice.

I laughed. I wanted it to sound mocking and cynical but I could hear the note of hysteria.

'Not very approachable!' I mimicked him. 'You sound just like my guardian. Dampen it down, don't let's get excited. We don't want any emotional outbursts, do we? Nasty frightening things, feelings. Let's have a nice safe intellectual discussion instead. Not very approachable! Christ! You're as bad as she is. And I used to think you were honest and not afraid of the truth.'

I was beating about on the lawn by this time and he was still lying propped on one elbow, but at my last words I thought I saw him shift as if in discomfort.

'Why can't you say straight out that she's scared to death of me?' I cried. 'She always has been, and it's worse now that I'm grown up. If I so much as raise my voice she imagines me going for her with the breadknife. It wouldn't be so bad if only she'd admit it. It's all this pretence, cover it up, hide it away, forget what your mother did – it's that that is driving me mad.'

I emphasized the last word by thumping with both fists on the grass. He sat up and it looked for a moment as if he was going to catch hold of my hands as he had done on an earlier occasion, but he seemed to change his mind and just looked at me instead.

'Mad,' I repeated, glaring at him. 'Mad like my mother. I suppose you're frightened of me too.'

He shook his head. 'No, Ruth, I am not the least bit frightened of you.'

Tears of relief sprang to my eyes; I blinked them back.

'That's a good thing,' I said, 'because I'm scared stiff of myself. I wouldn't trust myself for one minute with that breadknife when I get worked up. I'm glad you are here.'

'Yes,' he replied soberly, and something in the way he said it set my suspicious mind racing again.

'So that's it,' I cried. 'You're here to protect her, are you? How stupid of me not to have seen it before. But how tiresome for you. Aren't you neglecting your students and your duties?'

'A little,' he replied, 'but not irretrievably.'

I laughed. 'A keeper. A keeper for the lunatic. A man about the house in case she becomes violent. Not that it helped my father. It was my mother who did the shooting, you know.'

He did not react and I went on tauntingly. 'How long is this going to last? Are you giving up your job? Is she taking you on as a permanency?'

'Miss Murry is a fine, brave woman,' he said with great earnestness, 'but she has her limitations, just like the rest of us. She doesn't feel she can be of any further help to you at the moment.'

'Then why doesn't she send me away?' I said bitterly. 'She sent me away before. There are institutions for delinquents where they would no doubt keep my dangerous impulses under control. Why doesn't she take expert advice? Why doesn't she send me to a psycho-analyst if she thinks that is so wonderful?'

'We have thought of that,' he put in calmly.

I stared at him.

'You seem to have thought of a bloody lot, the two of you. Why on earth couldn't you tell me so straight away? Why all this roundabout business?'

'Because it's only a suggestion as yet. It depends entirely on your own wishes and on your co-operation. Any such treatment would be useless without.'

'I thought you didn't believe in it,' I said. 'I thought you said it was all nonsense. What about the lady in New York who told you you'd wanted to murder your mother?'

'Half-baked cocktail-party talk,' he replied. 'Properly qualified practitioners are quite a different thing. How do you feel about it, Ruth? Would you like to try to sort yourself out with such expert help? It will not be easy, but you aren't lacking in courage. What do you think?'

'What do you think yourself?' I countered.

'I think it's worth a try.'

'Whatever I discover about myself? Even if I turn out to have, to have – '

I could not utter my very deepest fear; it would sound too absurd. That I, as a small child, had in some way caused my parents' tragedy. A little girl of six. Bold and adventurous, but even so, how could such small fingers have had the strength to hold a gun? It was absolute nonsense and yet it had taken a firm grip on my mind.

'Even if I turn out to have been very wicked,' I concluded lamely.

'Even if you turn out to have been very wicked,' he said.

'And what about Nan? Does she think it's worth a try?'

His slight hesitation told me the truth; it was very difficult for him to tell a lie. Miss Murry was against my going to a psycho-analyst or to a hypnotist, or to anybody who might help me to recall the earliest years of my life, and it was he who had won her over to the idea.

'She wants what is best for you,' he said at last. 'She is only thinking of your good.'

'Oh, of course. That's why I was sent away from home to a strange place at the age of six just after the greatest shock of my life. That's why I was sent to a different school instead of to the one where the only person I loved and trusted was. That's why I was never allowed to visit my mother when she was alive. That's why it's all been kept a deadly secret. That's why I was told a whole packet of lies, or rather, of half truths, which is worse. Just enough to set my thoughts working, to build up my own edifice of horrors, but not enough to help me knock them down. Of course she was only thinking of my good!'

Suddenly my self-control deserted me and I caught at his arm and shook it as I had done on a previous occasion.

'Why did she do it?' I cried. 'Why didn't she just let me be? Why did she have to tell me anything at all? She could have made up any old story and I would have believed her. I had no reason not to. I remembered nothing.'

'She wasn't to know that,' he murmured, but I paid no attention for my own rhetoric was sweeping me along.

'Why has she tormented me so all these years? Giving me little glimpses and never letting me see the whole.'

He caught hold of my hands then, as he had done before, but there was nothing of excitement in it this time. It was simply to make sure that he held my attention, to stop me flailing about while I listened to what he said.

'Stop trying to account for other people's actions, Ruth,' he said. 'Concentrate on trying to understand your own. You must tell all this to the doctor. He has had a lot of experience as a neurologist with shell-shocked patients at one of the big London hospitals. You'll find him easy to talk to, and now that I know you're willing, I shall fix up an appointment as soon as possible.'

'Thank you,' I said. I was as weak and shaken as I always was after such an outburst but I summoned up the strength to add : 'That will relieve you of the burden too. You won't need to act as keeper any longer. You can go back to your nice quiet academic life and any wandering opera-singer who may happen to come your way.'

He burst out laughing and pulled me to my feet.

'Come on. Mrs Winter will be after us. The joint will be getting cold,' was all he said.

CHAPTER XIV

THE EX-NEUROLOGIST could not see me for several weeks and an appointment was fixed for early in August.

'Rotten luck on you,' I said to Miss Murry when she told me of the delay, 'having to put up with me for so long. Can't you dump me on some friends and give yourself a rest? Surely someone would take me in if you paid them enough.'

This particular piece of spitefulness was inspired by the discovery, made through some casual remark of my acquaintance the district nurse at Littleford, that Miss Murry had paid Uncle Matthew for my keep during the time I had lived in his cottage as a young child. Before my

recent illness I would have taken such a discovery in my
stride, but pneumonia followed by prolonged weakness and
depression had destroyed the resilience of childhood and I
was insanely sensitive to every little reference to my circumstances and upbringing. I searched for the worst possible
motives everywhere; I saw nothing but cruelty, neglect and
deceit; I believed myself to have been unwanted and disliked and, in so believing, became in truth more and more
hateful. Miss Murry suffered in patient silence. Mrs Winter
was less forbearing, and we had many a shouting match
when Miss Murry was out of hearing. Only with Professor
West did I behave tolerably, but he came less frequently to
the house during those weeks, having, as he said, a mountain
of examination scripts to shift.

At breakfast on my birthday, which fell that year on a
Saturday, I interrupted my guardian's painstaking attempts
to interest me in some form of celebration, by saying
abruptly : 'Isn't it about time I had my birth certificate?
You know they turned me down for nursing because I
couldn't produce one.'

It had become so easy to cause her distress that I did
not even trouble to look up at the result of my remark, but
just went on eating my egg.

'When was this, Ruth?' she asked.

'Last March, just before I fell ill.'

'If you had told me that you were thinking of applying
to train as a nurse,' she began carefully, as if picking her
way over rough and stony ground, 'then I could have – '

' – waved your magic wand and the way would have
been opened up for me,' I interrupted. 'Has it never
occurred to you that I should like to do something on my
own merits?'

'Has it never occurred to you that most girls of seventeen

or eighteen consult their elders about taking such an important step?' she retorted with a flash of spirit, but she spoilt it by adding : 'Girls of our type, that is.'

This was the cue for me to give an unkind laugh.

'Of our type! There speaks the champion of the classless society. Armchair socialists, lily-fingered revolutionaries, as dear friend Nicholas calls them.'

She poured out more coffee before she spoke again. Then she said quietly : 'It's your class too, Ruth.'

'But you pushed me out of it. Better a poor and honest workman's child than a high-class bastard. That's what you thought, wasn't it?'

The more I taunted her the more I hated myself, but I could not stop.

'Always the best of reasons for doing the wrong thing,' I went on.

'Yes, always.' She sighed. 'You shall have your birth certificate by lunch-time, Ruth. It's in my office at school. I have to go in to Oxford this morning to collect the mail and I will bring it back with me.'

'I suppose it's been kept in your file of difficult cases, problem children,' I said. 'Will you be handing the file over to this man who's supposed to straighten me out?'

'No,' she said, rather to my surprise, for I had not expected a serious answer, 'it's up to you to tell him what you like. He knows nothing whatever about you.'

It seemed to me that on this occasion, at least, she was speaking the truth, and since I could not at that moment think of anything else disagreeable to say, I remained silent.

'Would you rather I explained your circumstances to him?' she asked. 'Do you wish me to do that, Ruth?'

'I don't wish anything,' I cried, 'except that I'd never been born. As no doubt my mother did too, and my father, and you and everybody else who ever had anything to do with me. I was drowning, wasn't I? I expect I knew even then that everyone wanted me dead. Oh, why didn't you let me drown!'

'Do you want to come in to Oxford with me?' was all she said.

'No, thanks. I'm going to take one of the boats out. I think I'll row down to the weir.'

I wanted to frighten her. The weir was a notoriously dangerous spot for little boats, but she stood her ground heroically and did not flinch.

'Just as you like,' she said, 'as long as you're back for lunch at one. Mrs Winter wants to make something special for your birthday and you know what she is like when we are late.'

'I'll be back by one,' I promised.

As soon as she had driven off I began to wish I had gone with her to Oxford instead. I could have seen where she kept the birth certificate and perhaps caught a glimpse of other documents too. I might even have beaten her down into handing the lot over to me. What an opportunity missed, and all because I wanted to frighten her by hinting that I was contemplating suicide. Or was there still another reason? Was I still, in my heart, afraid to know?

I went down to the boathouse, stepped into the rowing-boat, and then instantly changed my mind and got out again. I was much too restless for the slow and measured motion of rowing. I stood for a few moments on the platform, trying to feel myself back into the scene of my father's death as I had so often done before. Nothing happened. It was as if the fever of my own illness had taken the ghosts away.

And yet I was full of foreboding. I wandered round the

garden and then returned to the house, but could settle to
nothing. I fetched my bicycle from the garage, got as far
as the front gate, and then turned back. The restlessness
increased to a pitch that was almost a physical pain. I
wandered about the house, opening one door after another.
Every room I went into seemed even more intolerable than
the one before.

When the telephone rang I slid down the banisters in my
haste to reach the hall to answer it. I was convinced that
it would be the police to say that Miss Murry had had an
accident. Appalled at myself, I yet longed for this to be
true. If something dreadful was about to happen, then let
it be quickly got over; let this suffocating, all-pervading
sensation of apprehension find relief in the shock of real
disaster.

It was Professor West, ringing to wish me a happy
birthday, and inviting himself to lunch.

'Are you all right?' he asked. I had gasped out the
number but had been incapable of saying more.

'I've just run downstairs,' I said, exaggerating my breath-
less state.

'Don't rush about too much this morning and tire yourself
out, Ruth,' he said, 'because we're going to the theatre this
evening.'

'Are we? Who is we?'

'We three, of course.'

Of course, I echoed bitterly to myself. Of course Miss
Murry could not be left out. But aloud I said : 'It's Shakespeare week, isn't it? What's on tonight?'

'*Hamlet*. A very good production, I'm told.'

'And very appropriate too. A most suitable tragedy for
my birthday. Isn't that just my problem too – to be or not
to be?' I laughed, too loudly. 'If only *my* father's ghost

would appear and tell me the truth!'

'Now stop that, Ruth,' he said. 'If you don't want to go I'll return the tickets and we'll do something else instead.'

I took a grip on myself and thanked him. There was no point in being ungracious, for I felt quite sure that before evening came something would have happened that made theatre-going quite out of the question. I went back to my aimless wandering after I had replaced the receiver, but it was less frantic now.

At about a quarter to one, when I had actually managed to spend ten minutes quietly looking out of the sitting-room window, I heard the sound of a car coming up the drive. Which one of them would it be? For a full minute I remained seated, revelling in the satisfaction of asking myself a question that would soon be answered, and then I got up and went into the hall. There was no one there. I opened the front door and saw Miss Murry's car parked in the drive, and at almost the same moment I saw Professor West's little two-seater turning in at the gate. He stopped just inside, jumped out and waved to me. I waved back, restraining myself from running to greet him with a hug as I had greeted Uncle Matthew when I was a child. He walked quickly down the drive, holding up a parcel, which I took to be my birthday present, for me to see, but as he came alongside Miss Murry's car he suddenly stopped and bent down.

It was only at that moment that I realized she was in the car, slumped over the steering wheel. My eyes had been on Professor West from the moment I saw him and had taken in nothing else.

He straightened up and called to me: 'Come here a moment, Ruth, I think she's ill.'

I came reluctantly, my whole inside twisting over with

fear. She had excellent health and I had never known her to spend even half a day in bed. If she was ill now, if she was dying, it was I who had brought it to pass.

Professor West pulled the car door open. She raised her head and gave a little sigh.

'Is that you, Nick?' she murmured. 'Just give me your arm to the house. It's nothing serious. I had a little shock – nothing serious but it rather upset me. I'm a little giddy. It will soon pass.'

He helped her out of the car and I watched in fear.

'Bring my bag, please, Ruth,' she said, 'and the parcels on the back seat.'

I picked them up and we moved slowly into the house. Professor West asked if she had had an accident and she shook her head without speaking. Nothing more was said until she was leaning back in an armchair and he was pouring her out a glass of brandy.

'Stupid of me,' she said with an attempt at a smile. 'It's only some news that I heard at school. Not unexpected and yet it has rather shaken me up. I'll be all right in a minute.'

She sipped at the brandy and then said: 'Don't look so scared, Ruth. I'm not dead yet.'

Thank God, I said to myself, but I could not say it aloud, not even at this moment, so hopelessly confused and contradictory were my feelings towards her.

She sipped again and her face began to lose its greenish tinge.

'I can get upstairs now,' she said, 'and I'll be ready for lunch in ten minutes, if you'll tell Mrs Winter.'

She got up slowly and took her bag from the coffee table where I had placed it.

'I haven't forgotten, Ruth,' she said, taking out a long envelope. 'Here it is.'

Professor West's eyes were upon us as I took the envelope from her. Does he know what it is, I asked myself; have they spoken together this morning? Did she get him to ring up in order to make sure that I was all right?

'Thanks,' I said and our eyes met. She had to look up to see me; I was several inches taller than she was now. 'I hope,' I said, and realized that my voice sounded menacing although in fact it was for reassurance that I craved, 'I hope the news that upset you had nothing at all to do with this?'

She put a hand to her forehead as if to steady herself against a fresh wave of giddiness.

'No,' she said, 'it's something quite different. To do with a pupil.'

She swayed a little and Professor West jumped forward to take her arm again.

'Shall I come up with you?'

It seemed to me that he spoke with most affectionate concern. But he can't possibly care for her, not really care for her in that way, I said to myself. The envelope with the precious document inside it remained unopened in my hand and I stared after them as they moved to the door.

'Thank you, Nick,' she said. 'I'll be all right now. I won't be long.' Her voice faltered as she went on :

'Stay here with Ruth. She may – need you.'

I thought : she is generous and unselfish, she is telling me that I need not fear her as a rival. And almost instantaneously I thought : she is doing this to show him how wonderful she is, how even in shock and sickness she can act perfectly.

He shut the door behind her and turned round and came towards me and I knew in an instant from the look on his face that I had no rival.

I backed away in fear; there was too much feeling; I could not contain it.

'Do you know what this is?' I asked, holding the long buff envelope out with both hands as a barrier between us.

He shook his head. 'No, Ruth.'

'Didn't she tell you?'

'No.'

'It's my birth certificate,' I said. 'I'm eighteen today. Old enough to make my own decisions. Old enough to get married. I asked her for it and she brought it to me. I don't see how that can have made her ill, do you?'

'No, Ruth, I don't see how that can have made her ill.'

He spoke very earnestly and stood absolutely still, recognizing the barrier of the envelope.

'It's more likely to make me ill, isn't it?' I went on. 'Not that it's going to contain any surprises for me.' I felt my voice shaking and I held my breath a moment and then went on, emphasizing every word as if I were beating myself with them : 'Ruth Redman, spinster, gave birth to a female child, father not stated, on the twenty-ninth day of July nineteen-hundred and fourteen. That is what it is going to say.'

He raised both arms as if to take hold of mine and then let them fall to his sides and shrugged his shoulders.

'All right. That's what it is going to say. So you are illegitimate. We all know it. If I were an American I would add : So what?'

'So everything!' I cried. 'Just you dare to tell me it doesn't matter that I'm a bastard. Just you dare!'

'I most certainly would not dare.' He began to laugh. 'I wouldn't presume to challenge a fury in full flow. Why don't you open the envelope? Perhaps you'll have a little surprise after all. Perhaps she had another Christian name.

Perhaps she was called Ermyntrude. Or Scheherezade.
Perhaps anything.'

I glanced up at him and had to smile in spite of myself.
Still keeping my eyes on his face I pulled up the flap of the
envelope and felt for the contents.

'Here comes the skeleton in the cupboard,' I said, 'here
comes my murky past.'

We laughed together and for the first time in my life I
had a clear vision of a future, a vision so glorious that it
almost took my breath away. Love and companionship and
truth in overspilling measure after years of loneliness. He
would say he was too old for me, of course; my only worry
would be to convince him that he was not.

'Hurry up, girl,' he said. 'Get it over. Take out the rotten
old skeleton and rattle it and then we can go on to sensible
things like opening your birthday presents.'

'All right,' I said, still looking at him and not at the
papers that I held in my hand.

It was at that moment that I realized something was
wrong. The paper that I was pulling out of the envelope
was too thin. It felt like a folded sheet of poor quality
writing paper and not like the stiff parchment of a legal
document. I looked down at last. It was indeed a folded
sheet and the typing showed faintly through from the other
side. I turned the envelope over and for the first time really
looked at it. It was addressed to Miss Annette Murry at
St Margaret's School. In the top right-hand corner was a
brown stamp; in the top left-hand corner was typed 'Private
and Confidential'.

My mind worked slowly. If she had put it in an envelope
for safe keeping there would be no address and stamp on it;
it would be marked, if anything, simply 'Birth Certificate'.

Perhaps it had remained in the envelope in which it had
been posted from the Registrar's office. But how clean it had
remained for eighteen years!

My eye went to the brown stamp again and at last my
mind registered the truth. It wasn't an old stamp at all.
The familiar profile of King George V was half hidden by a
postmark that clearly showed the date of yesterday. I looked
up at Nicholas and saw behind the big glasses eyes as
troubled as I knew my own to be.

'She must have given me the wrong envelope,' I cried.
'This came through the post today. It must be the one with
the news that upset her. I wonder if she's realized her
mistake. She said it was nothing to do with me, but – '

I broke off. A little cold voice of certainty was telling me
that yet again she had not been speaking the truth. No
pupil's affairs could have distressed her to the point of
collapse; nobody's affairs could so affect her, except perhaps
those of Nicholas or of myself. And he was here safe and
sound and as devoted to her in his own way as she could
ever hope him to be.

So that left only myself.

' – but I know it is,' I concluded, pulling the folded sheet
out of the envelope.

'Don't read it, Ruth!'

Nicholas sprang forward and caught hold of my wrists.

'Why not?'

'It's not addressed to you.'

'But it was given to me. Let me go.'

'She made a mistake.'

'Funny mistake. Accidental-done-on-purpose mistake. Let
go.'

'Please, Ruth. Let me look at it first.'

CHAPTER XV

WE LEFT Mrs Winter looking after Miss Murry and lamenting over the ruined birthday lunch, and drove off in Nicholas's noisy two-seater. In spite of the bumping and rattling I spent the first part of the journey in a semi-coma, barely conscious of who I was, who I was with, and where I was going. At one point I actually dropped right off into dreams. I was driving with Nicholas along a steep mountain road and all the world and its glory opened up in a great plain before us; but in the next instant I was shut up in a tiny dark place and the face of the nightmare came out at me and I awoke in suffocating horror.

'Are you all right, Ruth?' asked Nicholas.

'Yes. No. I think I might be better if I tried to keep awake.'

'All right then. We'll talk. What d'you want to talk about? Shall we have a frightfully academic discussion about Shakespeare's dark comedies? Or would you rather come nearer home?'

'I'd much rather have the academic discussion,' I said, 'but I don't think I can manage it at the moment.'

I pulled myself up in my seat and looked around me, trying to shake off the nightmare. We were driving through rolling green country broken up by loose stone walls.

'Where are we?' I asked.

'In the heart of the Cotswolds. We've at least another couple of hours' driving, I'm afraid. It would have been quicker by train, but this way we are more free.'

'Free, free,' I repeated. 'She has been there for twelve

years, shut up. Anything but free.'

'We're coming to the escarpment,' he said, ignoring my remark. 'The hills come to an end with a sudden drop and you see right across the plain of Gloucester.'

Like in my dream, I thought, but aloud I said : 'Did you really not know that my mother was still alive? Didn't you even suspect?'

'I sometimes thought Nan was holding something back,' he replied, 'but it was only a vague suspicion, based on no firm evidence. Whenever she consulted me about your future she held firmly to the facts as she had told them.'

'Held firmly to the lies she had told, you mean,' I said bitterly. 'It's a pity she couldn't have told an even bigger one. It's a pity she didn't tell me that my parents were killed in an accident and stick to that. That would have been courage, that would have been something to admire! To tell one whopping great lie and hang on to it against all comers.'

'Yes,' he said, and his voice was very troubled, 'but in a sense, you know, that is exactly what she did. Unfortunately she broke down under the strain. A weaker mortal would have cracked long before. I'd never have stuck it out myself. And yet — '

I glanced sideways at him and could see that his face was puckered up as it always was when he was puzzled. His thoughts were never far from the surface; he was no good at deception.

'And yet what?' I asked.

'I still don't feel that we have got to the bottom of it. She was worried to death. It can't be completely accounted for by having been caught out in this lie.'

'It can't indeed,' I agreed. 'She's scared stiff that I may find out something else and I believe I can guess what it is.'

'What is it?' He waited for me to reply but I said nothing. 'Well, come on, out with it,' he said sharply.

I wished I had held my tongue because I was not sure whether it was my genuine belief or only another of my fantasies about my parents and my past, but he continued to press me and there was no going back.

'I think she's kept me away from my mother because she's afraid I might learn something from her,' I said at last. 'I think Nan was much more deeply involved in my father's killing than she has ever let on. She knows something she's never told me and never told the police or the lawyers. Something even the housekeeper didn't know. Something only my father and mother knew. And my father was dead and my mother was mad. So her secret was safe. And now my mother isn't quite so mad and the secret is safe no longer.'

Nicholas pulled the car in to the side of the road.

'Why are we stopping?' I asked.

'To look at the view and because I don't like the sound of this,' he replied. 'So you think Nan Murry was involved in your parents' tragedy. How do you think she was involved?'

'I think she shot my father herself,' I replied. In spite of all my efforts I could not control the trembling in my voice.

'That is a very serious accusation,' he said. 'Have you any evidence for it?'

'Yes. No!' I cried. 'I don't know.'

I was twisting restlessly about. I felt trapped. The wide sunlit landscape meant nothing to me; darkness and terror were closing in. He caught hold of my shoulders.

'Listen, Ruth. This is serious. I mean it. If this theory of yours is based on anything other than fancy, then you had better tell me at once.'

'Oh, you and your evidence,' I cried, trying to escape.

'Yes, me and my evidence. It's very important. You'll never be a scholar if you don't know the value of evidence.'

'I don't want to be a scholar.'

'Yes you do. I'm not having you wasted. Now come on. What gave you the idea that Nan Murry was involved in your father's death?'

'It's only a hunch,' I said sulkily. 'Even scholars rely on hunches sometimes. You've told me so yourself.'

'True. But normally all that is at stake is the murder of an academic reputation. It isn't a matter of life or death. Can't you see the difference, Ruth?'

He was pleading with me now, and was no longer brusque and bullying.

'Oh, all right,' I said at last, still sulky, 'I know I imagine things. You would yourself in my position. I've probably imagined this. I'm only going on the evidence of her character and of her feelings. I happen to know them pretty well and I'd have thought you would know them too.'

I broke off suddenly. I had nearly said : she's hopelessly in love with you, it's plain as daylight; she always falls for clever men much younger than herself; she was in love with my father too. I don't know whether it was to save him embarrassment or whether it was from a remnant of loyalty to Miss Murry, but somehow I managed to catch myself up in time.

'I'm sure she's concealing something that she thinks I may learn from my mother,' I concluded lamely.

'A fair enough supposition,' he said with impatience. 'We are agreed upon it. I believe I hinted at the possibility myself a few minutes ago. But it doesn't get us very far, does it, and if that's all you have to say then we'd better be moving on.'

The sharpness pulled me round, as well he knew it would, and helped me to keep both calm and fully awake for the rest of the way.

'I've never been here before,' he said as we drew near to the village from which the institution of Longheath took its name, 'but I've had occasion to visit both a prison and an asylum at one time or another and this will no doubt be very similar. I'm afraid we must be prepared for something rather grim.'

'I know,' I said, 'I'm quite prepared for it.'

But while the place was of course nothing like the hideous Bedlam of my imagination, it was far more shocking, in a drab down-to-earth sort of way, than I had expected. We drove through acres of common land covered with bracken until we came in sight of the building – a huge, square block of dirty whitish brick. It stood there at the end of the road, at the end of the world, blotting out the sky : a great grey tank of despair. At each end of the roof was an open tower within which hung a huge bell. To deafen the countryside if someone should escape, I thought, and felt a sickening contraction in my chest. I must have uttered some sound, for Nicholas glanced at me.

'The bells,' I muttered. 'Horrible.'

'Yes, I know,' he said. 'Try not to look at anything. Try to shut out all reaction from your mind. Don't waste your strength on irrelevant things, but save it for your mother. You'll need every bit of composure that you can muster, but you'll be all right. You're going to visit your mother in hospital. Do you hear me, Ruth?'

He leant closer.

'In hospital. You've been in hospital yourself. There will be corridors with brown tiles, and wards and nurses, and a great smell of disinfectant. It won't be very pleasant but there's nothing uncanny about it.'

He stopped the car.

'Don't look around you,' he said, helping me out. 'Just hang on to me. I won't let you go. Just keep on saying to yourself that you're going to visit a patient in hospital.'

I did as he said. I clung to his arm and kept my eyes upon the ground. Voices came and went; doors opened and shut. We moved along. The ground turned from dark brown linoleum to scrubbed red tiles, then to bare wooden boards and it was suddenly very hot as if we were in a greenhouse.

'We're going out to the women patients' wing,' murmured Nicholas in my ear. 'It's not all that bad. The staff are quite human.'

I ventured to raise my eyes a few feet from the ground and saw the glass walls of the passage in which we were walking, and ahead of me a long black skirt nearly trailing on the floor.

'What's that!' I cried, clutching at Nicholas again. So busy was my fearful imagination that I believed if I looked farther up I should see the faceless black-clad figure of death herself.

'It's all right, darling.' He gave the ghost of a laugh. 'It's only the chaplain. Father Michael. Nice old boy. Luckily it's his visiting day and the governor suggested he should come along with us and be there when you see your mother.'

'Oh, I am a fool!' I cried, and I looked right up, and the figure in black turned round as he pushed open the door ahead, and I saw a plump pale face with pince-nez and I managed to smile at it.

'Come,' he said gently, 'come. You are doing a good deed, my child. I hope you will have your reward. I hope that on this day her mind will be clear and that she will know her daughter.'

'It's my birthday,' I said. 'I'd have come before. I wanted
to come and see her before, only I never knew – I was not
allowed – I was never told – '

I could say no more. I was choking and my eyes were
brimming over. Nicholas said something to the chaplain
and he held out a hand and said again : 'Come, my child.
We understand.'

I knew he didn't understand. I knew he thought I had
kept away through cowardice and distaste and shame and
not from ignorance. I knew Miss Murry had deceived
the prison authorities just as much as she had deceived
me, and that the chaplain was welcoming me now with
Christian forgiveness and understanding for my own weakness and my neglect of my mother.

I turned to Nicholas and looked up at him and opened
my mouth to protest. But he shook his head and held up a
hand and shook that too and there was no misinterpreting
his silent insistence that I should keep silent. So we walked
on into the hospital, and it was just as Nicholas had said
it would be except that the tiles were dark green and not
brown. Once I heard loud moaning, but that too might
have been heard in any other place of sickness.

We stopped at some big double doors painted the
same dirty green as the tiles on the walls, and waited. The
chaplain spoke about the improvements that had taken
place since his appointment and about how the inmates
were treated with greater humanity than before. Nicholas
answered him civilly, and in the midst of all my apprehension I felt angry with them both, standing there chatting
amiable generalities while I was approaching the crisis of
my life. But they could not have done otherwise.

Nicholas's hand gripped mine; the chaplain interrupted
his remarks to turn to me and say : 'Take comfort, my

child. You are doing right. You will treasure this moment when you did not fail her.'

They were good kind men, the one whom I knew and loved so well, and the stranger who represented God's love, and yet I had never in my life felt so utterly alone.

At last they were joined by another – whether man or woman I could not at first tell. I was conscious only of a dark navy uniform and a deep voice and a rattle of keys. I moved closer to Nicholas and drew in my breath. There came the sound of stiff doors being opened and then we were moving again.

'She's at this end of the room,' said the deep voice, and I realized then that it was a woman's, 'we keep the worst cases here, near to the entrance and the service rooms.'

We moved a few more steps forward. I kept my eyes low. I saw only a forest of black metal legs of beds against the green flooring. There seemed to be beds everywhere, all down the walls, all down the centre of the high room into which we had come, and along the narrower entrance way in which we stood. And there were sounds – whimpering, moaning sounds, like those of wounded animals; and an indescribable smell – disinfectant fighting hard to win the battle over something yet more pervasive – the smell of humanity decaying into death.

I was struck by a nausea so violent that for a moment or two I lost all sight of my purpose and could think only of the relief that it would be to breathe fresh air once more.

'Oh,' exclaimed the deep voice of the woman who was escorting us, 'they've put a screen round the bed. I hope this doesn't mean – '

She left the sentence unfinished and went to investigate. I looked up at Nicholas in unspoken inquiry and saw that his expressive face was tight with pity and strain. For a very brief moment I jumped outside myself and into his own feelings.

'Thank you for coming,' I murmured. 'I'm sorry to bring you to a place like this.'

'I go where you go,' he whispered back. 'Whither thou goest, to quote an earlier Ruth.'

The uniformed woman returned to us.

'It's all right,' she said. 'She is conscious, but restless and rather confused, I'm afraid. Is this the daughter?'

I let go of Nicholas's hand and stepped forward; my voice seemed to come from a very long way away.

'I am her daughter,' I said. 'Please may I see my mother now?'

'Try not to excite her,' said the woman. 'Keep very calm and see if she recognizes you before you speak. We have tried to tell her that you were coming but we can't be sure that she took anything of it in.'

'I understand,' I said.

With a doubtful look at me she drew the end of the screen aside. It was a dark brown screen, about six feet in height. Nicholas, standing behind me, could almost have looked over the top. I stood gripping the black iron rail at the foot of the bed and slowly raised my eyes.

I saw the coarse grey blanket, saw the wide border of a turned-down sheet; I saw a white gown, like a shroud, with stick-like arms protruding from the sides. My eye travelled up and up and I saw crumpled pillows and against them and sticking up above them so that it showed up against the dark brown of the far end of the screen there was a head. A head covered by red hair streaked with grey, shooting off in all directions like the picture of Shockheaded Peter, and underneath it wild eyes stared crazily from a blotchy face.

I gasped and swayed and the room turned upside down and my whole world dissolved in chaos. It was the face in the nightmare. The face in my nightmare was my mother's face.

I shut my eyes. 'No. It can't be. It must not be.'

I opened my eyes again and the face was still there. It moved, it stretched itself on the scraggy neck; it uttered sounds.

'No, no, no!' I shrieked. 'It mustn't be!'

There were murmurs behind me and the deep voice said sharply: 'Control yourself. If you can't control yourself you'll have to go.'

I closed my eyes again and when I opened them the fat face of the attendant was leaning close to the face on the pillows and the voice was speaking in a hideous travesty of a bedside manner.

'Wakey, wakey. Wake up, dearie. Here's your daughter, your little daughter come to see you. Isn't that nice now? Isn't that nice?'

I let go of the bed rail and stepped sideways. An arm closed round my shoulders and held me as I moved towards the head of the bed. I stood there with my arms hanging by my sides and steeled myself to look once more upon the face.

'Mother,' I said, 'it's Ruth. I've come to see you. They said you were ill. Mother, it's Ruth. Don't you remember me?'

I tried to lift my hand to touch the stick-like fingers but could not force myself to do so. I ought to kiss her, I thought; I ought to bend over and kiss that nightmare face.

I glanced round for the chaplain. I wanted to ask him, do God and duty ask me to do this too? — but at that moment the face came violently to life and the thin arms flailed against the bedclothes.

'It's no use now, she's off again,' said the attendant impatiently. 'Come along. We'll have to go. I'll get them to give her a knock-out dose.'

'Come on, Ruth,' said Nicholas's voice behind me.

But I lingered long enough to see the features grow more and more distorted and to hear the high voice shrieking. I thought I caught the words 'killed her' repeated several times and I shook off the comforting arm and returned alone to the head of the bed.

'It's me, Mother, it's Ruth,' I said loud and clear. 'I didn't drown. I'm here, alive and well. You pushed me in but I didn't drown.'

'What's this?' cried Nicholas, and the chaplain uttered a prayer, and the attendant said sharply: 'Come along now, leave her alone.'

But I ignored them all and leant over the bed, saying between the screams: 'You tried to kill me but you didn't succeed. I'm here. Your daughter Ruth. It's me. It's really me.'

The screaming and the flailing stopped. The eyes stared at me, growing larger and larger; the mouth fell open and strange gurgling sounds issued from it. Then suddenly there was an ugly choking noise and the whole stiff body collapsed and slumped sideways.

'That's torn it,' said the attendant, pushing me aside. 'Oh well, it's probably all for the best.'

'Come, Ruth,' said Nicholas in my ear.

'Come, my child,' said the chaplain. 'It's all over now.'

'All over?' I looked at them stupidly. 'Is she dead? Have I killed her?'

And then the room turned upside down again and I cried: 'Let me out – let me out – I'm going to be sick.'

CHAPTER XVI

AFTER THAT it was all confusion. There were more tiles, dirty cream this time, and an even stronger smell of disinfectant. Somebody held something to my lips and somebody bathed my forehead. Time passed, and then I was seated on a hard chair in a place with lots of people. They had strange faces and strange voices and I could not make out why they kept looking at me. At last one of the voices that did not seem so strange came close to me and said:

'We'll go now, Ruth, if you're feeling well enough.'

'Go?' I echoed. 'Go where?'

'Home, my dear. There's no cause to stay here now.'

'Home,' I repeated. 'Go home?'

While I was still puzzling over this I was raised to my feet and moved forward. The familiar voice spoke again:

'It's very kind of you, sir, but I think we ought to go. The sooner she gets home to her guardian the better.'

This made some sort of sense, but it still felt as if he was talking about somebody else. I felt my own lips move again:

'Is that all? Is it all over?'

The arm behind me guided me along. We left the tiles and came out into a bright light. We walked down some steps; we stood on a hard grey surface. I looked down and saw wheels and a long black garment nearly touching the ground. This time it did not make me shudder. There was no fear now; there was nothing at all.

The plump chaplain held my hand in both of his.

'Goodbye, my child, and God bless you. You will put all

this behind you. You have courage and ability. You have a fine useful life ahead.'

He turned to Nicholas.

'She's going up to Oxford, did you say?'

'We hope so,' replied the voice that I knew well. It sounded full of distress. Something seemed to be breaking up inside me again and I could not understand it because there was nothing left to break.

We got into the car and turned round in the courtyard. I looked back at the great grey building and began to feel a little pain, as if after all there was yet more to be torn away.

'Have we got to go?' I asked Nicholas.

'Don't you feel well enough?'

I shook my head. 'It's not that. I want – I want – '

He waited for me to go on, but I could not explain that I wanted us to be arriving all over again, wanted to be back in the nightmare so that I could hope for a different end. But the grim prison asylum had lost its quality of horror; it was nothing but an ugly old building where a handful of hardworking officials were doing their best for human wrecks who had nowhere else to live and die. It was the end of their road and the end of mine, the last place on earth where I could seek for re-birth, for a glimmer of love from the woman who had given me life. She was dead and there was nothing left. And yet I could not bear to leave this desolate spot that held the death of my hopes.

'I know why they go on embracing the corpse, why they jump into the grave,' I said to Nicholas.

He understood me at once. 'Hamlet,' he said, 'and countless humbler people too. We cling to the last physical remains. You know, Ruth,' he added, 'the chaplain said you were to come back for the funeral service if you wished.'

'No, no,' I said wildly, 'what's the use of that? It's all over. I'll never find her now.'

Again he looked at me in great distress.

'What's the matter?' I cried. 'Do you think I'm going mad?'

'I think we'd better move on,' was all he said. 'We've got a long drive ahead.'

For a while we proceeded in silence. There was nothing but the movement of hedges and trees and fields slipping by. At first it lulled me and stopped me thinking. I counted the telegraph poles, but after a while I kept losing count and began to worry about it. Then I found myself looking for faces in the shapes of the trees and the clouds. I was myself a tree-face with a grinning mouth and staring eyes and the wind waving the branches for the hair. We passed through a wood that was full of faces. We ground up a steep hill and came out among the fields again. I tried to recapture the soothing effect of the movement, which gave an illusion of escape, but in vain. Everything else was moving, but I was going nowhere. I was stationary in a spinning world; I could not get out of it. I seemed to be everywhere and at the same time I was nowhere; there was nothing left of me except thoughts that I dared not think. I could endure it no longer; I had to bring it to an end.

We were driving at a good speed along the top of a ridge with a steep slope dropping away to our nearside. Suddenly I stretched out a hand and caught hold of the steering wheel and pulled it round sharply to the left. There was a frightful bumping and screeching and we zigzagged from one side of the road to the other and in the midst of it all I could hear Nicholas swearing. We spun round and came to a halt tipped over the top of the grass verge overhanging the steep slope. With a great roaring of the engine Nicholas managed to back the car on to the road again. Then he heaved at the brake and turned to grab at me.

'Are you out of your mind, girl?' he shouted.

'I suppose I am,' I said, shocked for the moment into calmness. 'Can you wonder? I only want to be dead.'

'Well I don't!' he yelled. 'And I don't want you dead either. You mean too much to me.'

'I'm sorry,' I said. 'I can't seem to stop myself.'

'Look, Ruthie,' he said, holding me close, but I felt nothing for I was numb and nerveless, icy through and through, 'look, my dear, you're in a state of shock. You need expert care. We'll soon be home. You'll rest and you'll recover. It will pass. All this will pass.'

'Never,' I cried. 'There's nothing left. It will never pass.'

'Nonsense,' he said briskly. 'Don't be so dramatic.' But I could hear him mutter under his breath: 'What on earth shall I do with her?'

He felt about under the dashboard and produced some toffees.

'Here, chew some of these. It's something to concentrate on.'

I chewed obediently. It did indeed seem to help a little. He started the car again and moved forward slowly, every now and then glancing anxiously at me.

'I'm sorry to be such a nuisance,' I said. 'I'll try not to do that again.'

But I was still wondering how I could escape him, so that I would not have to risk his life while making an end of my own. When we came to the next town, I thought, I could say I wanted to find a public lavatory. It steadied my mind a little, to worry at my plan, just as chewing the toffee eased the trembling of my lips. He must have suspected my intentions, for on the outskirts of Gloucester he stopped the car and got out the Thermos flask that the staff at Longheath had filled for us and offered me the sweet strong tea. I pushed it aside. It tasted of life, and all I wanted was to grow colder and colder and die.

'It's pretty foul,' said Nicholas, drinking from the cup that I had rejected, 'but better than nothing.'

To my surprise I found myself resenting his matter-of-fact voice and the fact that he did not press me to drink. He replaced the Thermos and lit a cigarette.

'I need a break,' he said. 'I'm shutting my eyes for a few minutes but that doesn't mean you are not to talk if you want to.'

All of a sudden my plan of escape to suicide seemed rather melodramatic and absurd. He knew me so very well; he had detected the small signs of recovery in me.

'What am I to talk about?' I asked.

'I believe I heard you say to your mother,' he replied, 'something to the effect that she had tried to kill you but didn't succeed. Did I hear rightly, Ruth?'

I tried to speak but felt as if I was being strangled. He threw away his cigarette and put an arm round me.

'Please, darling, don't try to run away from it any longer,' he said. 'You've come all this way. You must see it through now. You remembered something when you saw your mother, didn't you?'

'It was very upsetting,' I muttered. 'I must have been wrong.'

He scolded me gently. 'And this is the girl who was so determined to find out the truth at all costs, who was so ready to blame other people for concealing it. Shame on you, Ruth. Are you going to turn aside now? Come. Tell me. What picture came into your head when you saw your poor mother?'

'She threw me into the water,' I whispered. 'She told me that she wanted me dead.'

'I see. That would explain a very great deal. Are you absolutely sure?'

'I'm quite quite sure,' I replied. 'I don't need any hypnotist or psycho-analyst to bring it back to me. It all exploded in my mind when I saw her face. She screamed at me and hit at me again and again while I was drowning. That is perfectly clear. And there was someone in the background shouting, perhaps trying to stop her. That part is not so clear but I know it happened. It's a shadowy figure but I know it was there. It might have been Nan. Or it might have been my father. Is this — ' my voice began to shake again — 'is this good enough evidence for you?'

His only reply was to hold me very close and call me his dearest Ruth again and again. I heard the words and I felt that he was warm and alive and I believed that he cared deeply for me. But it all meant nothing. The icy numbness was upon me again. I drew away a little.

'I wish you'd stop trying to console me,' I said coldly. 'It isn't any good. I wasn't intended to live. Even my own mother wanted me dead.'

'Stop thinking of your mother,' he cried eagerly. 'Stop thinking of the past. Think of the future. Think of all those who love you.'

I turned my head aside and I thought I heard him sigh.

'Think of Nan,' he went on, 'try to imagine what she must be feeling now. You asked why she didn't tell one big lie and stick to it against all odds. Isn't that just what she did? She kept from you the knowledge that your mother had tried to kill you. She made it possible for you to believe that your mother had loved you. She saved you from such a scene as we have just witnessed. Perhaps she ought not to have tried, but it was a brave effort and it cost her very dear. All these years, carrying her burden of knowledge all alone, putting up with your resentment and your abuse of her. And always fighting with her own doubts – was she doing right? would you ever discover?'

I drew away from him. He was pulling me back to life and I didn't want to come.

'She needs your love and pity,' he went on. 'All these years of trying to protect you, are they to end with a call from the police telling her you've met with a fatal accident? Is that to be her reward? Do you really want to punish her so much?'

'Oh stop it, stop it!' I cried, unable to listen any longer. 'You've made your point. Why do you have to go on tormenting me like this? Haven't I had enough? I can't stand any more, I tell you. I can't stand it.'

We stared at each other for a moment and then I looked away.

'If I promise that I won't try to do anything at all until we get back to Rivermead,' I said, 'will that satisfy you?'

'It's some comfort,' he said grimly, and set the car in motion again.

I leaned back with my hands lying loosely in my lap and for the first time since we had left Rivermead I felt the relief of tears stinging my eyes. The fields, darkening now, slid past, and the strange melancholy of the countryside in the twilight was heavy upon me. But the crazy impulses born of the sight of my mother had quite died away and been replaced by a more rational anguish. I saw Nan Murry as we had left her – pale, exhausted, defeated. I could hear my own voice shouting at her, reproaching her. I remembered every bitter word I had said to her and my mind lingered on them with shame.

L

'I do hope she is all right,' I said.

'She is all right,' said Nicholas wearily. 'I telephoned from the governor's office. Mrs Winter answered.'

'You think of everything, don't you?' I said, with an attempt at my old easy manner towards him.

He did not reply and I glanced sideways at him. There was still light enough for me to see the expression on his face. His mouth was dragged down as if in grief or pain. It seemed to be making some silent demand on me, his own unhappiness, and I could not face it now. I took refuge in attack :

'I suppose you thought if you got me worried enough about Nan it would take my mind off myself and I'd stop trying to smash us up,' I said.

'Shut up and go to sleep,' he replied.

Surprisingly enough, that was just what I did, and this time I had no dreams. I awoke when we turned the sharp corner into the drive of Rivermead. The moon was full and the house cast long shadows over the lawn that led down to the river. I put a hand on Nicholas's arm and felt it stiffen.

'It's all right,' I said. 'I'm not trying any more funny business. But I'd like to stretch my legs round the garden before I go in.'

'All right,' he said resignedly, leaning across me to open the passenger door, 'we'll stretch our legs then. Just for a minute.'

'You don't need to come,' I said. 'I'd rather be alone.'

He gave a small exclamation in which I read exasperation and something else that I didn't want to know about. I deliberately pulled down a shutter in my mind to exclude all that was alien to my mood.

'Don't worry,' I said as I got out of the car. 'I'm not going to drown myself. I only want a moment to come to terms with it all before I see her. She'll understand.'

'All right. I'll tell her then,' he said, and again I shut my mind against that note of pain.

I had walked several yards across the lawn before I realized that I had not even thanked him for all he had done for me that day. I turned back to the drive, but the car had moved on and he had gone into the house. For a moment I stood hesitant, wondering whether to follow. And then I turned my footsteps back to the moonlit lawn. My thanks would have to wait; at this moment Nicholas had no place in my heart and mind. The very thought of him disturbed my mood.

It was a strange mood, unlike anything I had ever experienced before. There was great sadness in it but there was also the relief of calm after storm; and a certain nostalgia, as if I had lost something very precious; but at the same time a feeling of acceptance, of resignation to my fate. I walked slowly across the lawn and looked back at the house, outlined against the calm moonlit sky. My eyes lingered on every gable, every piece of guttering, every chimney as if I were seeing them for the first time. It was a kind of ritual re-birth, an emergence from a chrysalis, the coming to consciousness of my new self.

For a little while I stood savouring this unfamiliar quietness of mind and then I moved towards the boathouse, confident that my new-found serenity would stand the test of what I was going to do. Even in the happiest times of my life, when the shadow had shrunk to its smallest, I had still felt some uneasiness when approaching the boathouse. I had worked hard at my boating and my swimming partly to get over this feeling. But tonight all apprehension was gone. I opened the wooden door and stepped into the dank darkness. This was the heart of my ritual. I was burying the past. I stood on the platform and looked out through the open end of the hut to the moonlit water and the trees on the opposite bank. And then I said softly aloud:

'Now, memory, do your worst.'

It all rushed at me then, the shouting and the terror; the distorted face with the staring eyes and the wild hair. I saw it as it must have been when it happened, in the semi-darkness of the little building on a bright autumn evening, the shadows giving it an extra dimension of fear. I had clambered over the boats and had hidden behind the back-rest of the punt when I heard them come in. They had been quarrelling as they came through the door. It was not strange to me; I had often heard it before.

'You can't go to India! You're not to go!'

That was my mother, raving like a fury. And a man's voice had replied: 'We can't go on like this.'

'Then I'm coming with you.'

'Don't be absurd,' came the reply. 'You can't come with me if we aren't married. The Army is not like the theatre. And anyhow, what about the child?'

Of course my memories did not bring back the actual words; I was re-creating the scene for myself, filling out my childish perceptions with the fuller understanding of my adult mind.

'Damn the child, damn, damn the child!' screamed my mother. 'I wish she'd never been born. A millstone round my neck. Ruining my life, losing me everything I care for. I wish she was dead!'

A short tense silence and then a sound like a slap across

you must, but don't be harsh to him. He of all people has done you no harm – unless loving you painfully and believing himself too old for you to return his love can count as harm.'

'Please, Nan, I can't think about it tonight,' I cried in exasperation. 'I can't. Why do you have to start talking about Nicholas now?'

'It was you who mentioned him,' she said.

I had no answer to this. I said goodnight for the last time and left the room before the tension between us became even greater. I got into bed and lay there trying to recapture my earlier mood of serene acceptance of my own history and all that had gone to its making, but it would not come back. The horrors of Longheath and my mother's death and my own state of mind on the journey home were all things of the past, but my mind was a jangle of irritation with Nan and self-reproach for not being more patient with her, and real deep guilt towards Nicholas for letting him go away, unhappy and unthanked, after he had carried me through this great crisis of my life.

In vain did I tell myself that it was not many hours till the morrow and I would make it all up to him then. At two in the morning I had hard work to restrain myself from running downstairs to telephone him. The hours passed very slowly. At half past three I got up and leant on the window-sill and looked out at the mild summer night in an attempt to quieten my restlessness. But my mind raced on and on. Of course I loved Nicholas, but I couldn't endure to discuss him with Nan. She was playing her old game again, showing how noble she was by making it clear that she was renouncing all claim to him. She was directing my life as much as ever, handing Nicholas to me on a plate. It was past dawn when I fell at last into an unquiet sleep, which

lasted only a short while, and before Mrs Winter was
stirring I was already up and dressed and wandering about
the garden, chewing over all that had happened the previous
day and longing for Nan to be up so that I could make a
fresh attempt to come to terms with my resentment of her.

'Do let me make a fuss of you,' I said to her several hours
later when she came out to sit on the lawn. 'It would make
me feel less mean about having been so beastly to you all
these months.'

She laughed quite gaily and my spirits rose.

'What can I bring you?' I asked. 'Cushions, sunshade,
tea, lemonade?'

For a few moments we were both quite happy and at ease
with each other. Then we fell silent for a while, and after
debating in my mind how to get on to the subject of my
mother without too grating a change of key I said at last :
'I believe we were sitting on this very spot when you first
told me about my parents after I came back from Uncle
Matthew's. Do you remember, Nan?'

'Yes, I remember. You were making daisy chains – working away at them as if your life depended on it. You made
three. Two of them looked like handcuffs and the other
looked like a hangman's noose. It was uncanny and horribly
appropriate. I remember thinking at the time that child as
you were, and although you seemed to have forgotten what
you saw, yet in some extraordinary way you knew that your
mother was connected with a killing. It was then that I
decided you would have to be told at any rate part of the
truth.'

'It feels now as if I have always known it all,' I said.
'Which I suppose in a confused way I have. But there's just
one point that I'm still not clear about and I wish you

would clear it up for me now. If it's not too much effort
for you to talk, of course.'

'I want to talk,' she said. 'I want to get this straight.
What is it in particular that you don't remember?'

'What happened after my mother pushed me in. But
perhaps you can't help me. You see,' I added almost
apologetically, 'I still don't know what part you yourself
played in the whole business, Nan.'

She sighed. 'I think perhaps I had better tell you exactly
what I saw and heard and what I did from the first moment
I knew that something was wrong.'

'Please,' I said gratefully.

'I was standing here, just about where we are now,' she
said, 'when I heard the first shot. It took me a moment
to realize what it was and where it had come from, and it
puzzled me because I knew your father had no revolver
with him. He had joined the regular army and was being
posted to India, but he was on leave then and not in
uniform. Later, of course, we learnt that your mother had
got hold of it some time during the war and had hidden it
away. When I reached the boathouse Julian had leapt into
the punt and it had shot away from the raft and was
rocking about violently from side to side. Your mother was
blocking his way. He called out – forgive me, Ruth, but I
must tell you everything now – he cried, "You murdering
bitch, get that child back." And he called her filthy names
and flung her aside. Then either he overbalanced in the
swaying boat or else she tripped him up, and at the same
moment I tripped in the rowing-boat. I was climbing across
it to get to the punt, you see. I looked up to see Julian lying
on his side across the edge of the punt, with one arm gripping the back-rest and the other arm stretched out over the

water. And I saw your mother pick up the revolver which had fallen to the bottom of the boat when Julian tripped, and she steadied it with her other hand, and as he twisted round and reached out farther in order to pull you to safety, she shot him through the heart.'

'I see,' I said softly, 'I hoped that was it.'

'Hoped?' she repeated, puzzled.

'He might have thought first of retrieving the revolver,' I explained. 'But he didn't. He thought first of retrieving me.'

'That's true,' she said. 'How strange. I never thought of it in that way.'

'And if he hadn't tried to save my life,' I went on, 'he might not have lost his own. He might have been alive now. And my mother might never have gone mad.'

I very nearly added: 'And how different my own life would have been,' but I stopped myself in time. No reproaches or regrets, that was my resolution.

'What did you do next?' I asked.

'I called out to her from the other boat: "Put that thing down, Ruth." And I pulled the rowing-boat towards the punt and climbed into it.'

'With her pointing a loaded revolver at you!' I exclaimed. 'Good God.'

It was my turn to be surprised. In all my earlier imaginative reconstructions of the scene I had never pictured Nan herself facing acute danger, so skilfully had she minimized her own part in it.

'Well, yes,' said my guardian. 'But she did put it down, you know, and then she collapsed completely and lay there moaning, and I had to climb over her, and over your father's body, to get to you. But by the time I had pulled you out of the water, Mrs Morrison had come, and I was able to hand you over to her while I got your mother into the house, and we didn't have long to wait for the doctor and the police.'

'Did you tell the police what you have just told me?' I asked.

'Well, not quite. There was no need for them to know that your mother had pushed you into the water. With all that fighting going on it was very credible that you had fallen in of your own accord.'

'I hope you didn't tell them that my father pushed me in,' I cried, the words jumping out before I could stop them.

'No. They weren't all that interested in how you got there. The main point was to establish whether or not your mother had shot in self-defence. If that could be proved, it would save her from hanging.'

'But you knew she hadn't shot in self-defence,' I said, starting up again in fresh suspicion. 'You knew she killed him when he was lying defenceless in the bottom of the boat.'

'Oh yes,' she said. 'Of course I had to tell them that.'

I subsided with a grunt of relief.

'It was very difficult to know what best to do,' she went on. 'It is a terrible responsibility to take, to swear away another person's life. Even a stranger's, let alone a girl who has been very close to you, as your mother had been to me.'

'I suppose so,' I murmured. 'Yes, I can understand that.'

'You see, it was not immediately plain that your mother could not be considered responsible for her actions, and in spite of the fact that I was able to give instances of her instability, they did actually initiate a trial for murder. Fortunately, however, it was soon established that she was

unfit to plead. Try to put yourself in my place, Ruth. Try
to imagine what my feelings must have been, when I could
look on your mother's incurable insanity as a bit of good
luck, as a deliverance rather than a terrible misfortune.'

'Oh, I do understand,' I cried, 'indeed I do. But if you
needed to show that she was mad, wouldn't it have been
additional evidence to say that she had been trying to drown
me?'

It was a long time before she gave me an answer, and
when she did it was in an indirect form and in her best
lecturing voice.

'It seemed to me,' she said, 'and it still does seem to me,
that for a child to know her own mother has tried to kill
her is a blow to the psyche of such magnitude that it must
put that child's whole future development into jeopardy.
Particularly when the child has been through such very
traumatic experiences and when there is a history of mental
disturbance in one of the parents to start with. This
knowledge, I decided, would have to be kept from the child
at all costs.'

She turned upon me a look that moved me deeply and
confirmed me in my resolution.

'Did I do wrong, Ruth? It has not been easy for me.
Did I do wrong?'

'No,' I cried, 'a thousand times no. You did wonderfully
right.'

'In spite of all your doubts and questionings and the
horrible way in which you learnt the truth at last?'

'In spite of all my doubts and questionings and the
horrible way I learnt the truth at last,' I repeated. 'I was
strong enough to take it then. I wouldn't have been strong
enough before.'

I pressed her hand and lifted it to my lips. I had spoken

with great emphasis and I think she believed me. There was sincerity between us at last, of feeling if not of fact. If she could tell a lie and stick to it heroically because she believed it to be in my own best interests, then the least I could do was to perform a similar service for her. But when I leant back in my chair again I had to turn my head aside to hide the tears that had sprung to my eyes. I honoured her decision and admired her fortitude, but I believed her to have been terribly wrong. How different my life would have been if only I had known the truth! I would not have exhausted my youth in fruitless fantasy, I would have been spared the horror of yesterday that had for a short while taken away my own reason. Truth instead of falsehood, certainty instead of doubt, the vision of a hand stretched out to help me instead of the vision of a nightmare face.

It was this last that I resented the most. She had robbed me for all these years of the great healing knowledge that one of my parents had cared that I should live, and had offered me instead a shaky edifice of lies. If only she had realized that I could have conquered the fact that my mother had tried to kill me if only I had known that my father had tried to save me. Why had she not understood this? Why was she so reluctant to give any credit at all to my father?

Reproaches sprung to my lips and I fought them back. Instead I said brightly : 'What an experience for you, Nan. I can't get over how brave you were – rushing into a gun battle as if it were a dog fight. You know, I suspected all along that you were much more involved in it than you let on. I made up all sorts of stories about it. My most recent one was – oh no, I can't tell you. I'm too ashamed.'

'Coward,' she said laughingly.

'All right then. But don't be angry. Not knowing what

really happened, you know, I was bound to set my morbid imagination to work. I thought you were hiding some dreadful secret. I decided that you had shot my father yourself and had planted the deed on my poor mother who was not in a position to deny it. You see how crazy I was.'

I smiled at her and she tried to smile back but I could see it was an effort.

'Where on earth did you get that idea from, Ruth?' she asked.

'Oh, I just made it up. But you didn't like him, did you, Nan? Julian, I mean. My father.'

'I'm sorry, my dear. I'm afraid I did dislike him intensely.'

'Any particular reason?'

'He ruined your mother's life. Though admittedly she did ask for it. But otherwise, no, no particular reason.'

She's lying, I said to myself. This is the lying voice. She was in love with him herself. She made a fool of herself over him and he was probably absolutely beastly to her and hurt her pride dreadfully.

'I'm sorry, Ruth,' she said again.

I looked up and smiled. 'Don't worry, Nan. I quite understand. My father was an utter swine. I quite realize that.'

'Yes,' she said.

'My poor mother. What a man to fall in love with. And he wrote several bad plays and just one good poem.'

I quoted a few lines from those I had learnt years ago from the anthology of war poems. Nan was amazed.

'How on earth did you find that out?' she asked.

'Instinct, I suppose. Isn't it extraordinary? Unless he had it in his mind and perhaps said some of the lines aloud when he was playing with me. I suppose he did sometimes come and play with me? Uncle Matthew seemed to think so, and I think I have some sort of misty memory too.'

'Yes,' she said reluctantly. 'He did know how to amuse a small child. It was his one redeeming feature.'

'Just one more question, darling Nan,' I said, 'and then I will release you from a topic that I can see is distasteful to you. Has he any relatives living? Or rather, I ought to ask, are there any relatives who would not be revolted and scandalized if the daughter of the woman who killed him got in touch with them?'

'I feared that was coming,' she said. 'Oh well. I suppose it doesn't matter now. I will tell you about his wife's family some time if you feel you have to know, but of course you must not get in touch with them. It was much too painful for them all. But there is a brother. I had some correspondence with him at the time of Julian's death. He is a housemaster at a public school. He never had much use for Julian and his main concern was to hush up the scandal. But it's a long time ago and people are less rigid about these things nowadays. I don't think he would object to your getting in touch provided you approach him delicately. His name is Peterson. Francis Peterson. It used to be Petrovich – Franz and Julius Petrovich. They were of Eastern European origin, but they were brought up in England and naturalized, and they changed the names long before the outbreak of war. You must not mention this, of course, to Mr Peterson.'

It took me some minutes fully to take in these revelations. 'So I am half foreign,' I said. 'How strange.'

And then a few moments later: 'And I've got an uncle. An uncle! A real, live, true uncle!'

I jumped to my feet. I knew it would distress her to see my bounding excitement, but I did not know how to contain it.

'It's nearly lunch-time,' I said. 'Shall we go and have my birthday glass of sherry now?'

It was impossible to keep still. It was excessively difficult to contain myself over lunch and chat to her about subjects that I knew would interest her, when all the time I was overwhelmed by the need to talk to somebody about the wonderful news that I had a living uncle of my very own. Mrs Winter was no good; she was too close to Nan. But as soon as Nan had settled down to a much-needed after-noon rest I got out my bicycle and pedalled away at a great rate along the Oxford road.

All other doubts were set at rest in the great certainty that there was only one person with whom this newly identified Ruth really wished to share herself.

CHAPTER XVIII

It was quite a long ride, for Nicholas's new house was on the northern outskirts of the city, beyond the area of vast Victorian and Edwardian mansions where both St Margaret's School and Freelands School were situated. I had not yet seen it, but he had promised to invite Nan and myself as soon as he had had time to sort out the muddle and to engage a daily woman to clean for him.

It was in the last of the side roads before the great new by-pass that was now nearing completion, and it looked very raw and bleak after all the leafy gardens and weathered brick past which I had ridden. A square box of a house, standing in a patch of rough grass outlined by a wire fence. It looked more like the sort of place a prosperous tradesman would choose, and for a moment I felt quite angry with Nicholas for not putting himself into a setting that would do him greater justice. Evidently I was not the only one to be unsure of my standing in relation to other people. Nicholas was still uneasily straddled between his working-class childhood and his adult status, and in choosing himself a permanent home he seemed to me to have made the worst of both worlds.

The old two-seater stood near the front door, on the rough stone track that at present served as a drive. At least that meant he was at home, and I was about to knock when I suddenly changed my mind and decided to try to steal on him unawares. We are all of us different beings when we are alone, and I had a great longing to see Nicholas for a moment as his solitary self. It would help me to make up my own mind. The main living-room was at the back of the house, I found, and on this hot day the french windows stood wide open. I crept along close to the wall until some of the room came into view. There were shelves reaching to the ceiling, with books lying on them in untidy piles, and there were many more piles on the floor. I inched forward and saw the corner of a desk, similarly laden, and beyond it the side of a brown leather armchair. Hearing no sound, and growing bolder, I stepped right in front of the open window so that I could see into the room and for a few moments, but those were enough, I had a clear picture of Nicholas alone.

He was slumped back in the chair, marking examination scripts. I could see great heaps of them on the floor by his side, in their blue-grey covers, and as I watched he wrote something on the one that lay at the top of the small pile on his knee and threw it down to join the others. Then he laid his pen on the wide arm of the chair, took off his glasses and rubbed over his eyes and forehead as if he had a headache, replaced the glasses, picked up his pen, and turned over the cover of the next script.

I must have been blotting out some of the light as I stood in the window, but he hadn't realized it; he thought the dimness was in his tired eyes. I put my foot on the step, making a slight noise, and he looked up and stared at me, not with surprise or annoyance, but with weary indifference.

'Hullo, Ruth,' he said. 'Is Nan with you?'

'No, she's resting. She's still very tired. I came on my bike.'

'Sorry I didn't ring this morning to find out how you both were. I meant to ring, but – '

He waved a hand languidly to indicate the confusion in the room.

'Have you been working all night, Nicholas?' I asked.

'There wasn't all that much of it left, was there?' he said with a faint burst of irritation. 'No. I haven't. Only since about nine o'clock this morning.'

'Have you had any lunch?'

'Not yet.'

'Mind if I bring you some? Has your Mrs Whatsername started coming yet?'

'Not on Sundays. But she's left some bits and pieces.'

He was already hard at work on the scripts again before I was out of the room. To my relief, the kitchen was well equipped and in tolerable order, and so were the other rooms into which I looked. I had seen the worst first. I heated up some soup and put it on a tray with some cold meat and salad and an apple and returned to the study.

'Thanks, Ruth, very kind of you,' he said briefly.

'It's the least I can do, after yesterday,' I replied. 'Not to mention all the other days when you've been coping with my hysterics instead of getting on with your work. Are you very much behind? Can I do anything? Checking marks, or packing, or anything?'

It turned out that there was a lot of checking and counting to be done and we worked for some hours. I had not been so contentedly active since I had looked after Uncle Matthew.

When all the scripts had been disposed of into sealed parcels, I looked round the room and said: 'Now to get your books in order. Where shall we start?'

But he would not let me do any more. 'I've got a couple of students coming in tomorrow to help,' he said. 'Don't want to turn down their offer. Besides, I'm whacked.'

'I'm not surprised,' I said.

He lay back in his chair and shut his eyes and I wondered if I ought to go. I had gladly postponed the telling of my own great news, but I could not help feeling disappointed at having to put it off for yet another day. I washed up the last round of teacups, returned to the study, stood by his chair, and said softly: 'I'll be off now, then, if there's nothing more I can do.'

He stretched out a hand and caught hold of mine. 'Thanks, Ruth.'

'Thanks to you,' I said. 'For yesterday. And everything. Goodbye then.'

'Goodbye,' he said, but did not let go my hand.

I waited a moment. He was leaning back, quite relaxed, with eyes closed again. I could not make out what he really wanted me to do and had almost decided to perch myself on the arm of the chair, which I could do without disturbing him, when the telephone rang.

'Damn,' he muttered. 'Do answer it, Ruth. It's in the hall.'

A few moments later I came back and said : 'It's Elaine Bailey. She wants to know if you're free tonight. She's having a few friends in.'

'I'm not free,' he grunted.

'Shall I go back and say so?'

'Say anything you like.'

I returned to the telephone and had a verbal skirmish with the gushing lady at the other end. She was obviously dying to know who I was, and I was feeling jealous enough to enjoy frustrating her.

'Who is she, Nicholas?' I asked when I came back again to the study.

'A don's wife. A North Oxford hostess. Gives Sunday evening soirées where they pick to pieces each senior member of the university in turn.'

'It can't be your turn, then, or you wouldn't be invited.'

It had been clear from his voice that the lady was no old secret flame of his. My little spurt of jealousy died away.

'You'll be dissected tonight, though, all the same,' I added, laughing. 'She was terribly intrigued to hear a female voice, and one so obviously very much at home here. Gosh, I should like to be a fly on the wall in Mrs Bailey's house this evening.'

I bounced up and down on the arm of the chair and shook him.

'Wake up, Nicholas! Put your mind to it. How are you going to explain me away?'

'Impossible,' he said, 'it'll be all over the town.'

'I might be a sister.'

'They know I haven't any.'

'Or a cousin.'

'Cousins are suspect too.'

'A secretary, then.'

'On Sunday afternoon? At home? Some secretary.'

'Housekeeper? No, I don't think I sounded like a house-keeper. One of your students. That's it. A young lady from Somerville. Sounds like a limerick. There was a young lady from Somerville, Who thought her professor was wonder-ville, So she struggled all day, To induce him to say, That he too was in love with – with – with . . . oh hell, it doesn't have any rhymes! Why didn't I pick on an easier college? But that'll do, won't it, Nicholas darling? You're duty-entertaining a gaggle of female students. Might that do?'

I glanced at his face and thought I saw a slight twitch of the lips, but he replied very gravely : 'It might do if it still happened to be term time. But it's not. They've all gone down. The lads who are coming tomorrow are staying up for part of the vacation to do some extra reading.'

'Oh.' I sobered down a little. 'Does Mrs Gossip Bailey conduct her character dissection sessions in the vacation too?'

'This will be the last. They start again in October.'

'Heavens! How does she manage without it all those weeks!'

'In any case it won't wash. I heard you on the phone. Nobody could possibly mistake you for a student. Nor for anything else either. What the hell were you playing at? Why did you have to change your act halfway through and put on a foreign accent? It sounded like a bad amateur production of *Die Fledermaus*. Why all this phony Hungarian countess stuff?'

I burst out laughing.

'Because, for all I know, I may be one. Because I'm only

half English. Because my ancestors came from Eastern Europe.'

I threw my arms round his neck and kissed him.

'No inhibitions,' I said. 'Like your New York lady. I'm half-foreign. I'm allowed to do anything.'

'Ruth, Ruth,' he said, holding me away from him and looking at me in amazement, 'would you mind telling me what this is all about?'

'My father was not quite a gentleman,' I babbled on, 'in fact he was a pretty average specimen of the genus cad. But I've got an uncle – do listen to this, Nicholas! – I've got a very respectable uncle. He's a housemaster at a public school. There! What do you think of that? That brings me up to your level, doesn't it? One English public school housemaster of slightly dubious origin set against one English university professor of very humble origin. I reckon we're quits, don't you?'

He was looking at me in the way he had looked when I had been about to tear open the wrong envelope. There was pity and pain and a great deal of love.

'In fact I'm not sure that I'm not one up on you,' I added. 'I reckon my uncle will think it is he who is doing the condescending when he comes to give me away at my wedding. Oh yes, I'm going to have a proper wedding – the full works. In the cathedral. Do you think illegitimate children are allowed to get married in cathedrals? I don't see why they shouldn't, do you? Nothing could be more legitimizing than a cathedral wedding. And then we'll scandalize the lot of them. We'll give Sunday soirées and invite all those unfortunate ladies who've had their eyes on you hopefully for years. They'll have a wonderful time picking me to pieces, and saying it won't last because I'm much too young and flighty for you. Poor man, how sadly he's been taken in.'

I said my last words in a genteel old lady voice and then raised my arms to put them round his neck again, but he stepped back, and I had to let them fall to my sides. For a moment I stood there feeling horribly deflated, as if I had been taking a great bounding run to clear a high jump, only to find the obstacle was not there after all. Then I sat down at the desk and took up a pen and prodded at the blotter.

'I'm sorry,' I muttered. 'I seem to be making rather a fool of myself. I seem to have misunderstood you. I suppose you are always telling young ladies from Somerville and elsewhere that they mean a lot to you. I suppose most of them are too sophisticated and sensible to take it seriously.'

I dug through the top layer of paper and started on the one beneath. My face was burning and I dreaded hearing him speak. But even worse than the shame I felt at having offered myself and received no response was the horrible doubt that I had been trying all night to suppress and that had still been there, I now realized, underneath all my posturings. I loved Nicholas and my gratitude to him was beyond telling. He had given me back my chance to live, when I had come to the end of my own strength, not once but again and again. There would never as long as I lived be anybody else, man or woman, for whom I could feel such depth of love and gratitude. But I did not want to marry him. I thought of Mrs Bailey and all her friends and the sort of life I must lead if I married Nicholas and I knew in my heart that it was not for me and never could be. All my bubbling about had been a great big cover up, trying to deceive myself as well as him.

The silence went on and on. I would have bitten out my tongue rather than speak a word to hurt him now, but I knew that he would see through it in an instant if I tried any more pretence. My head drooped lower over the mutilated blotting paper. The silence became intolerable. Shall I go into hysterics, I thought? Shall I do a faint? I had just decided to look at my watch and exclaim in horror and say that I had to run, when I became conscious of a slight sound, the last sound in the world that I had expected to hear. I looked up and saw that Nicholas was laughing, not very loud but unmistakably laughing. He clapped his hands together lightly several times and then sat down in the big armchair.

'Bravo, Ruth,' he said. 'That was a fine performance. I hope you'll get the chance to repeat it before a larger audience one day.'

'It wasn't a performance,' I cried. 'I meant it. Every word.'

'Now come, come, child –'

'Don't call me child!' I interrupted, shrill with relief. It didn't matter what I said now; he was going to come to the rescue yet again.

'All right then, Miss Murry. Or Miss Redman, or Miss . . . what did you say your father's name was?'

'Petrovich. Anglicized to Peterson.'

'Ruth Peterson. No, I don't think it sounds very good as a stage name. I think you'd better keep to your mother's. It rolls off the tongue more smoothly.'

I stared at him. 'What on earth are you talking about?'

'Your future career. No, don't interrupt.' He held up a hand in a most authoritative manner. 'You've had your say. It's my turn now. I am giving up all claim to make a scholar of you. You'll train as an actress. You'll be a very

good one. You'll travel. You'll meet a great many people
of all different kinds. Everything will open up for you now
that you have truly found yourself. As the nice old chaplain
said – you've got a fine life ahead.'

'I don't know,' I muttered, once again prodding at the
blotter.

'Nan will raise no objection,' he went on, 'or rather, none
that I can't argue her out of. And illegitimacy is no draw-
back in the theatrical world. In fact you may not even need
to play the trump card of your eminently respectable uncle.'

It seemed to me that there was a hint of bitterness in
these last words and I stole a glance at his face. It looked
perfectly calm and unmoved and yet I did not think I had
imagined the slight restraint. Was it just that he wanted to
be the one who was doing all the giving or had he too been
having dreams of a future for us together? I knew that I
ought to leave it alone, but the little devil of inquisitiveness
that had been with me all my life drove me on :

'Do you really think that I ought to go on the stage?' I
asked.

'I do indeed.'

'But what about . . .'

'What about myself? Well now, I suppose I may be
allowed a moment of madness. Men of my age are rather
subject to such aberrations, I believe.'

'You're laughing at me again,' I protested.

'Seriously, Ruth, it wouldn't do. You know it wouldn't.
But for heaven's sake, girl,' he added, coming over to the
desk and putting his hand on my restless ones, 'don't look
so miserable. We're not saying a big farewell for ever. And
I'm not going to die of unrequited love. If you are relieved
at escaping the prospect of an elderly husband, does it not
occur to you that I may be equally relieved at not having

to take on a flighty young wife?'

I glanced up at him again and this time I could detect not the faintest sign that he did not mean exactly what he said.

'It's not fair,' I complained, 'you're cheating me of my big renunciation scene. But you're not going to cheat me of this.'

I lowered my head and pressed my lips to his hand and kept them there a long time because it said what I wanted to say far better than any words could do.